Sheila reached out to Jennifer's hands, slowly turning and lifting them until Jen's palms were on Sheila's breasts. Jennifer swallowed hard. They continued to stare into each other's eyes. No smiles now, just the thick, heavy curtain of seduction lay between them as their pulses quickened and their breathing shallowed.

LINDA HILL

Bella
BOOKS

2007

Copyright© 1997 by Linda Hill

Bella Books, Inc.
P.O. Box 10543
Tallahassee, FL 32302

First Published 1997 by Naiad Press

First Bella Books Edition, August 2007

Editor: Lila Emspon
Cover designer: Sandy Knowles

ISBN-10: 1-59493-77-5
ISBN-13: 978-1-59493-077-5

To Barb

For that pristine morning nearly two decades ago
that changed both our lives forever.
I love you.

Acknowledgments

One of the truly surprising things to come from writing *Never Say Never* has been the overwhelming support and encouragement that I've received from family, friends, and especially from women and readers whom I hadn't met before its publication. To each of you, my sincerest thanks and appreciation.

Special thanks to my dad for his unwavering pride and enthusiastic support.

Portions of this story were inspired by my sister, Judy, and her family. Thank you, Judy, for being the glue that keeps us all together.

About the Author

Originally from the Midwest, Linda Hill now makes her home in the Boston area. She has yet to decide whether or not she'll attend her own twenty-year high-school class reunion.

Class Reunion is Linda's second novel. She is also the author of *Never Say Never, Just Yesterday, Captive Heart,* and *Treasured Past.*

Prologue

1970

"Come on, Jenny. Let's get out of here." Sheila Hoyt shuffled her schoolbooks to one arm and placed an impatient hand to her hip.

Jenny's twelve-year-old blond head swung around, her eyes finding Sheila's as she trotted up the field. Her cheeks were flushed, and she was breathing hard as she flashed a smile.

"One more," she called while holding up a single finger and pretending she didn't see the way Sheila rolled her eyes. She was the last to join the small group of boys that huddled together, several feet behind the football.

Johnny Shaw was outlining a play, telling Danny Johnson to run out toward the baseball diamond and then cut left.

"What about me? I've been open all day." Jenny knew that if Johnny would just throw the ball to her, she could score a touchdown. Nobody was covering her.

"Take the sideline. Straight out," he told her.

She caught the smirk that passed between Danny and the other boys but ignored it. After all, she was used to it. But if they would just give her a chance.

"Okay. Let's go." They clapped their hands and broke the huddle, each crouching down at the line of scrimmage. Jenny tugged up her skirt, pulling it high over her knees so that she'd be ready to run.

"One. Two. Three. Hike!"

The ball snapped and Jenny took off, Sheila's dark head a blur as she sped past on her way down field. Watching over her shoulder, she saw Johnny pumping his arm. She curled in toward the center of the field.

"I'm open! I'm open!" No one was around her, and she watched with determination as the ball spiraled through the air, just to her right.

She raced over, the cold air whipping her cheeks as she stretched her body, reaching out both hands for the ball.

In midair she felt her body slam against something hard, knocking her off balance as she fell to the ground.

"Shit!" Danny Johnson had grabbed the ball,

nearly falling as he stumbled over her. He twisted toward the sideline, his body colliding with another as his shoulder hit the ground and the ball shot from his grasp.

"Shit. Stupid girls!" Danny launched into a tirade as Jenny lifted a face hot with humiliation from the ground.

He sat several feet away, his legs tangled with arms that belonged to Heather O'Brien. The girl had somehow managed to wander into his path, and she was now sitting square on her backside, looking around like she didn't know what had hit her.

"You stupid idiot!" Danny was furious. "What are you doing out here in the middle of the football field?"

The fact was, Danny had run out of bounds as Heather had wandered by, her face buried in a book, totally oblivious to her surroundings.

Jenny picked herself up, noting the grass stains on her bare knees as everyone trotted back to their huddles. Everyone except Danny. He'd picked up the football and was glaring down at Heather.

"What's the matter, Four-Eyes? Did you lose your glasses?" he taunted. "Is that why you didn't see me coming?" He tucked the ball under one arm and hovered over her menacingly.

Jenny watched the scene, wanting to interrupt, but not wanting to draw attention to herself. Especially after she'd practically collided with Danny herself.

Heather's books were strewn everywhere. She was on her knees, squinting at the ground as she picked up several books. She was running her hands across the grass, searching for something.

Jenny could see that Heather was crying, her face bright red as she kept her lips tightly pressed together over the braces that covered her teeth.

Heather had Johnny's full attention now. He began ridiculing her in earnest as his voice grew louder. "Did you lose your glasses, Tracks?" He lifted one foot, pushed his sneakered toe against her shoulder, and sent her sprawling.

Jenny had seen enough. "Leave her alone, Danny," she said, her voice sounding braver than she felt. She sauntered over, squatting down beside Heather and reaching out a hand to help her up.

"Are you okay?"

Blue eyes, made bright from tears, turned to Jenny.

"My glasses," Heather said. "I can't see without my glasses." Her nose was bright red, and tears rolled down her cheeks. The metal braces on her teeth winked in the sunlight.

Jenny searched the grass with her, her hands and eyes sweeping out, but coming up empty. Her ears heard the crunch just as her eyes caught sight of Danny's foot grinding the spectacles into the ground.

"Oops," he drawled dramatically. "Guess I must've stepped on 'em." He grinned broadly as he lifted his foot. "Gee, I'm sorry, Tracks." His laugh was cruel.

"You're a butthead, Johnson." Jenny couldn't keep the words from slipping out. Her heart sank as she reached over to pick up the glasses. They were crushed. One lens was shattered, and one earpiece hung, uselessly bent.

She held them out to the other girl, hating the look of pain on Heather's face as she took the glasses in her own hands. Anger and frustration showed in

4

the cheeks that seemed to grow redder and redder. Then she lifted what was left of the spectacles into place on the bridge of her nose. She blinked hard and stared, eyes wide, right into Jenny's face.

Jenny knew the other girl was biting back angry words. She'd never seen Heather angry before. No matter how many times she'd witnessed the other kids laughing and calling her names, Heather had always simply dipped her head and walked away.

But this time Jenny could see the frustration and disgrace hot in her cheeks. Those startling blue eyes were staring, not at the cause of her torment, but directly into Jenny's gaze.

"I'm sorry, Heather," she muttered, watching as Heather's bottom lip began to quiver.

Jen's stomach hurt. She hated Danny Johnson. She hated him because he never let her play with the boys. And now she hated him even more. For crushing Heather's glasses. For calling Heather Tracks and Four-Eyes. For making those tears slide so easily down Heather's face.

Danny was laughing now, but he was losing interest in his game. He sauntered toward the other boys as he flipped the ball in the air.

"Hey, guys," he called. "Tracks lost her glasses!" Jenny's ears burned as she heard the hoots and taunting from the other players. "And would you believe she's even uglier without them? Phew," Danny continued at the top of his lungs. "We've gotta find something to cover that face up!"

Something inside of Jennifer snapped. Rage boiled and burned in her gut. Without thinking, she leaped to her feet and charged after Danny, hatred pushing her faster, until a growl burned low in her throat.

She vaulted high and onto his back, catching him by surprise. Satisfaction coursed through her veins as she tackled him to the ground with a loud thump. Then she was upon him, flailing her arms and fists wildly, knowing any contact was better than none at all.

"Fight! Fight! Fight!" Every kid left on the playground was upon them, chanting, howling, urging them on.

Jenny was vaguely aware that the skirt of her jumper was hiked up around her waist, but she didn't care. All that mattered was hurting Danny. He was no longer stunned, and his fists were flying out now, aiming for her face. She felt blow after blow begin to strike her, and she grew more determined. She closed her eyes, continuing to flail wildly.

Shouts of "Fight! Fight! Fight!" were interrupted by other shouts. "Teacher! Teacher! Teacher!"

Adult hands under her arms lifted her high and away from Danny's body. She struggled incoherently against her captor, but strong arms wrapped around her, holding her firmly.

"Jennifer Moreland! What do you think you are doing?" Mrs. Martin's sharp tone brought her quickly to her senses. Shame ripped through her body, quickly replacing the anger that had pushed her just moments ago. Of all the teachers at the grade school, Mrs. Martin was her favorite.

Mr. Schofield, the physical education teacher, was hauling Danny up by the collar of his shirt. "What are you doing? Fighting with a girl. You ought to be ashamed of yourself."

"Principal's office. Now, young lady." Mrs. Martin's voice left little room for interpretation, and

Jenny made a quick about-face and headed toward the school building.

The walk seemed to take forever. Jenny tried unsuccessfully to avoid one pair of eyes after another as she searched for Sheila. She knew that Sheila would be mad, but she wasn't prepared for the frown on Sheila's face — or the way she shook her head in disgust. But the final blow fell when Sheila simply turned away, holding schoolbooks firmly to her chest, and began the long walk home, alone.

Chapter 1

1987

Jennifer couldn't put it off a moment longer. As much as she wanted to turn around and march right out of the airport terminal, she knew she had to put one booted foot in front of the other and get on that plane.

"Final call for flight five-seventeen to Saint Louis. Passengers should now be onboard. This will be your final call." The flight attendant was looking right at her, eyes hard flints as they beckoned her to board the plane.

Jennifer grimaced, running long fingers through her short-cropped dark-blond hair and letting it fall back across her brow as she leaned over. She hefted a carry-on over her right shoulder while fishing for her boarding pass in the back pocket of her Levi's.

She returned the attendant's cool smile and bit her tongue when the shorter woman told her that the airline preferred passengers to board early if they were holding tickets in the higher row numbers. As if she didn't know the rules.

She made her way down the aisle, waiting patiently behind one passenger after another as they made last-minute adjustments to their carry-ons. Then she settled down in 32-C, thankful that no one was occupying 32-A, and that apparently no 32-B existed. She stretched out her long slender legs as much as possible, noting that the seat belt sign was already flashing. The plane began to roll away from the gate. No turning back now.

Why had she let her sister talk her into this trip? She hadn't been back to Des Moines more than four times in the past eight years. Even then, it had taken a death, a wedding, and two births to get her to return. A high-school reunion hardly belonged in the same category as those other events.

To say that Jennifer had misgivings was an understatement.

"But you'll have fun," her sister had insisted. "I had a fabulous time at my reunion. They voted me the one who had changed the most."

Of course Sally had had a wonderful time. Of

course she'd been voted the one who had changed the most. She'd transformed herself in ten years from a dowdy bookworm to a drop-dead, knockout, gorgeous female with a handsome, successful husband and two equally gorgeous children. Of course she'd had a fabulous time at her reunion. Everyone had fallen all over her. Every guy in the place must have wondered how they had ever let her slip through their fingers. *And I'll bet a few of the women thought the same thing too.*

"It's, uh, different for me," Jennifer tried explaining.

"But why?"

How could she explain it to her sister? *Because I went from being a nobody jock to being the only dyke in the entire high school.* With the exception of Diane Miller, of course. Now *there* was a bull dyke.

"Everyone will show up with their husbands and wives. They'll ask questions that I'm not sure I want to answer," she'd finally said.

There was a moment or two of silence on the other end of the line before Sally replied, her tone suddenly hushed.

"Nobody will know that you're *gay*."

Jennifer cringed as her sister emphasized the word. "Of course they will," she snorted.

"Well, how will they know? You don't have to *tell* them." Again the near whisper.

"I'm certainly not going to lie." Her feathers ruffled, Jennifer dropped her own voice low, mimicking her sister. "And I did live there, you know. I wasn't exactly a nun."

"You slept with someone here?" Sally's voice grew a full octave higher.

Jennifer rolled her green eyes. This was almost amusing. Almost. *"Yes, I slept with someone there,"* she whispered. An image of Sheila Hoyt flashed across her mind and she sighed, her voice returning to normal. "I'm sure it's made it through the grapevine by now. Des Moines just ain't that big," she drawled.

"Who? Who did you sleep with?" Sally demanded. Jennifer could hear the kids in the background, squealing and giggling. Is that why Sally was whispering? She didn't want the kids to hear?

"Nobody you know," she lied flatly.

"Oh." Her sister sounded disappointed. "Who cares what they think anyway. Just think about coming, okay? You never know. Maybe Sheila will show up. Do you ever hear from her?"

Jennifer went cold at the mention of Sheila's name. "No. Not in years," she said quietly.

"There you go. She'll probably be at the reunion."

"Probably," she agreed. *One more reason not to go.*

"All right, I won't tug anymore. Just think about it, all right? Tommy is nearly two, you know. You haven't seen him since he was born." There it was. The guilt.

"I'll think about it," Jennifer conceded, already trying to figure out how to arrange the time off from work. Guilt was a wonderful motivator.

The flight from Phoenix to Saint Louis would take a little over two hours. Once there, she would have a brief layover before the hour-long flight to Des Moines. Jen took a deep breath and settled into her seat. Closing her eyes, she tried to relax and ease the tension that was creeping along her shoulders.

Maybe her nerves were on edge for nothing, she

reasoned. Maybe the trip would be completely uneventful. *Not likely,* she thought, *too many emotional skeletons in the closet.* She thought of her sister and missed her in a wistful sort of way. When they were children, she and Sally were inseparable. Jen couldn't help missing her when she allowed herself to think about it. What had happened? They'd grown apart during high school. Sally was interested in boys and clothes and shopping, while Sally was interested in basketball — and Sheila.

Then Jen had moved away. Sally got married, and shortly afterward the kids began to arrive. Jennifer could swear that every conversation that she and Sally had shared over the past six years centered around Sally's children. Not that she begrudged her sister in any way. She was quite happy for her sister. But since Jen became a stumbling idiot whenever a child came near her, she found it difficult to relate to Sally. It wasn't that she didn't like kids; she simply was completely clueless about what to say to them.

Maybe this visit will be better, she mused. Allison was nearly six years old and in school. Surely the two of them could hold a real conversation by now. And Tommy was just beginning to talk. A quick pang of guilt gripped her. She'd waited too long to see Tommy again.

A male flight attendant was coming up the aisle, pushing a serving cart, and offering breakfast to each passenger. Should she be daring and go with the omelette? Jen peered over the shoulder of the gentleman in front of her and wrinkled her nose. The eggs looked pretty risky.

"I'll take the hotcakes." Her voice betrayed her

thoughts, and the attendant grinned as he handed her a tray.

Ever since that phone call from her sister, Jen had made a conscious effort not to think about Sheila Hoyt. Every time her image came to mind, Jen pushed it away, refusing to give it life. But now she let the memories come as she tried to imagine what Sheila might look like today.

She struggled to recall Sheila's nineteen-year-old body. Curves. Round hips. Large, heavy breasts. It was harder to recall that same body in its adolescent years.

Where Jennifer's body was board straight and narrow, Sheila's had always been curvaceous and full. It was easy to remember those curves now. And Sheila's breasts. Oh, the heaven Jen had known when her face was buried between those huge breasts.

She couldn't picture Sheila without them. Although she knew there must have been a time, because she could recall the first time she'd discovered them. They were playing *doctor*, as usual. They were in Sheila's bed, of course. They had no privacy at Jen's because she shared a room with Sally.

Jen was the doctor, as she usually was when they began this ritual.

"Hmm." She fingered the puffiness around Sheila's left nipple and nearly broke out of the doctor character. "Nothing to worry about, Miss Hoyt, although there does seem to be a bit of swelling."

"I told you, doctor," Sheila replied gravely. "What should I do?"

"Oh, I have just the medicine, my dear." She leaned over, lightly brushing her lips across first one nipple, then the other. She lingered, smiling as first one and then the other nipple began to pucker.

"There." Jennifer lifted her head and smiled at her patient. "I recommend similar therapy at least once a day from now on."

As always, Sheila began to squirm beneath her, already forgetting the game they were playing. Her young, thirteen-year-old body was pressing up against Jennifer, begging for attention.

Jennifer laughed. "You're always in such a hurry."

"I can't help it." Sheila grimaced. "I'm becoming a woman, you know, now that I have my monthly friend coming to visit."

Jennifer giggled at Sheila's imitation of Mr. Schofield, their physical education teacher. Mr. Schofield never talked about *this* when he talked about the girls becoming women in health class.

"Jenny!" Impatiently, Sheila rolled her over, pushing Jennifer beneath her as she pressed herself down, rubbing herself against the other girl until she finally sighed and rolled in a heap beside her.

"Coffee, Miss?"

"Huh?" Jennifer looked up at the flight attendant and grinned sheepishly. "Sure. Please. Cream. No sugar." She accepted the plastic mug and put it to her lips, nearly burning her tongue on the hot liquid.

Jennifer did her best to concentrate on the in-flight movie as the airplane continued its journey to Saint Louis. Once there, she chose to wait in her seat while other passengers boarded. Within moments, it seemed, the plane was once again in the air.

She stared out the window at the puffy clouds beneath the plane, trying to separate the memories of a child and the emotions of an adult. She didn't know if she loved Sheila or hated her. Of course, she'd loved her when they were young. But she hated the way it had turned out.

She couldn't really remember particulars anymore. She couldn't recall at what point they had stopped pretending to play doctor. She had no idea when they began saying *I love you,* or when every song on the radio seemed to be written especially for them. Just as she couldn't quite pinpoint when they had stopped planning to go to college together, or when they had stopped saying that they would be together forever.

All Jennifer could remember were the boys. One after another. Infiltrating their world. Suddenly Sheila wanted to go out with boys. *Because everyone will think we're queer if we don't.* She'd insisted that they double-date, and Jennifer always went along, copying Sheila's smiles and laughter, and even kissing the boys the way she'd only kissed Sheila in the past. She could vaguely recall the way that her stomach had fallen the first time she'd witnessed Brian Dunne putting his tongue in Sheila's mouth. And the first time she'd seen Bobby Grimes fumbling to grab at Sheila's breasts was the last time she ever put herself in that position.

Somewhere along the line she'd given up, even though nothing really changed when they were alone. It was almost as though Sheila were two separate people. The popular one who laughed and giggled publicly, and the private one who spun her magic around Jennifer whenever they were alone.

Eventually, Jennifer had gone away to college alone and Sheila had stayed in Des Moines and attended the local community college while she decided what she wanted to do with her life.

It wasn't until Jennifer had been away for about a month that she realized the real reason Sheila had stayed behind. It came in the form of Sheila's excited voice over the phone on a Monday morning as Jennifer headed out to class.

"Bobby asked me to marry him!"

"What?" Completely stunned, Jen was unable to fathom such an idea. "Bobby Grimes?"

"Of course Bobby Grimes. Who else?"

What a stupid question. Why would Bobby ask Sheila to marry him? Somehow she knew the answer, but didn't want to see it. "What did you tell him?"

"I said yes!" came the gushing reply. "Oh, Jenny! Can you believe it? We're getting married next spring! You'll be my maid of honor, won't you?"

Stunned into silence, Jennifer could barely squeak out a reply. "B-but, what about us?"

"What *about* us, silly?" Sheila smoothed things over. "Nothing's changed. We're still the same. But I want to get married. I want to have kids."

"Kids?" Jennifer whispered. Since when had Sheila wanted kids? Since when did she know Bobby well enough to marry him?

Sheila was rambling on, saying something about picking out her wedding gown and writing invitations. Jennifer couldn't decipher the words above the roar in her ears. Her knees were so weak that she had to lean against the desk to steady herself.

"I have to go, Sheila." She mumbled something about being late for class before dropping the receiver back on its cradle and eyeing it as though it were the devil himself. Her first instinct was to go to Des Moines and see Sheila face-to-face. But Arizona State

16

was a long way from home, and she was forced to wait.

She agonized for months, barely able to focus on anything except what she would say the next time she saw Sheila. When the Christmas holiday arrived, Sheila was true to her word. She treated Jennifer the way that she always had. They made love at every opportunity. Wildly. Playfully. The way they had those years ago when Jen was the doctor and Sheila the patient. But this time Sheila reversed the roles, seemingly determined to make some point, to control the situation.

They barely spoke of Bobby and the upcoming wedding. So that even as she tried on the peach satin bridesmaid's gown that Sheila's mother was patiently pinning together, she didn't believe for a minute that she would ever have to put it on for real. The wedding would never happen. She knew that Sheila loved her and that she just needed a little time. She would figure it out and never marry Bobby Grimes.

After lulling herself into a false sense of security, Jennifer returned to school with a different outlook. She began to concentrate on her studies, finding joy in the challenge of her classes. She began to reach out and make new friends, amazed to find how much she enjoyed meeting the diverse group of students that covered the campus. She began to think that the world and her eyes were opening up just a little bit more each day.

She soon found herself befriended by Georgette Hildibrand, a wild-haired sophomore who lived on the top floor of Jennifer's dormitory, whom everyone referred to as Georgie. Georgie was by far the most outspoken and flamboyant individual that Jen had ever met. She was outrageously funny, her manner frequently pushing the borders of good taste. Reluctant at first, Jen couldn't help but be a bit mesmerized by Georgie's teasing.

Originally, Georgie had approached Jennifer right after Christmas break, begging for help with chemistry.

"I failed the class last year. I have to get through it this time and I still don't know the difference between H_2O and CO_2." Wide green eyes pleaded with Jen. "Please help me. I'll carry your books. Wash your clothes. Anything."

Initially taken aback, Jen couldn't say no to the other girl. After that day, they met several times a week, going over and over the lessons from class. "You're amazing at this," Georgie would shake her head and say. "You should be a chemist or something."

Jen hadn't really thought about what she would do eventually. She used to think that she wanted to be a veterinarian, until her dog got hit by a car and her parents had to have him put to sleep.

"How about a pharmacist?" Having just walked back from the library, they were waiting for the elevator that would take them to their rooms.

"A pharmacist?" Jen wrinkled her nose. "Sounds kind of dull."

Georgie shrugged and laughed. "Oh, like you're just oozing excitement, eh farm girl?"

"I told you —" Jen began heatedly as they began the short elevator ride upstairs.

"I know, I know," Georgie waved her off. "You've never even been on a farm."

"Actually I was once." She motioned the other girl to follow her as she stepped out into the hallway of her floor. "I walked beans when I was ten or eleven."

"You walked beans?"

"Yeah," she shrugged as they stopped just outside of Jen's room while she unlocked the door.

Georgie began to laugh, clutching her long unruly hair and tossing it over her shoulder. "Wait a minute. Let me get this straight. You *walk* the beans?"

"Yeah. So what?" Jennifer glared at the shorter girl as they entered her room. They both dumped their books on the bed.

"What do you do?" Georgie grinned. "Put a little collar on them and drag them around?"

Jennifer grimaced, the butt of yet another of Georgie's jokes. "Very funny. Walking beans means walking up and down the rows and pulling the weeds."

"Yuck," Georgie blanched. "Physical labor. Sounds backbreaking."

Jen felt somehow vilified, admitting that it was. They decided to go out for pizza, and Georgie poked around the room while Jennifer changed her clothes.

"Is this your girlfriend?" Georgie held up Sheila's graduation photo.

"Huh?" Jen's eyes flew to the picture and back to Georgie several times while her cheeks turned bright red.

Georgie raised one eyebrow. "I mean is she your *girlfriend*. Your *lover*. You know."

Jennifer's jaw dropped. How did Georgie know? Was Sheila her *lover*? They had never given it *that* name before. And they had certainly never mentioned it to anyone else.

"Oh, don't be such a prude," Georgie misinter-preted Jennifer's reaction and scowled as she placed the photograph back on the bureau.

"No," Jen assured her. "It's not that. I just . . . Well, yeah. I guess she's my girlfriend." She smiled down at the other girl. "I've just never said it before."

"You never said it before?"

Jen shook her head. "How did you know? I've never told anybody."

"Oh, you know," Georgie shrugged. "I have a lot of gay friends," she winked. "It takes one to know one. Got it?"

Jennifer stared at the other girl, not quite com-prehending. She had never heard anyone say that they had gay friends before. In fact, the only times she had heard the word *gay* was when one of the kids referred to Charlie Little back home. The word was usually coupled with the words *queer* and *faggot*, and while Jennifer had some vague ideas about what the terms meant, she only really knew that she didn't want those words associated with her — par-ticularly when Sheila made a point of saying that she didn't want anyone to think they were *queer*.

"There're actually quite a few gay bars around here that we go to all the time," Georgie was saying. "Have you ever been to any of them? I could take you there."

Jennifer felt as though a thick fog was settling around her, like she was struggling to see through it but wasn't quite able to. Her mind reacted slowly, grinding through the information instead of sifting through it quickly.

"Gay bars?" Jennifer plopped down on the bed, spilling her schoolbooks to the floor.

"Yeah." Georgie joined her on the bed, crossing her legs as she gazed at Jennifer's oddly vacant look. She tilted her head to one side as she tried to interpret her friend's reaction. Then she playfully slapped Jennifer's knee.

"Oh, don't worry. Women go there too. Most of the clubs are pretty mixed. But there are a couple of dyke bars too. But if you want the truth," she wrinkled her nose, "they're really more into the butch-femme thing. I'm not real comfortable there." She stopped short and stared at the other girl's blank stare. "It's okay if that's what you're into, though. I could take you to either place."

Jennifer began to slowly shake her head. *Dyke.* Everyone had called Diane Miller a dyke.

"Hello?" Georgie slapped her knee again. "Talk to me, girl. I feel like I'm digging myself into a hole here."

Bewildered, Jennifer continued to shake her head. "Georgie. You're confusing the hell out of me. I don't have a clue what you're talking about," she admitted.

"You're kidding me, right?"

Blushing, Jennifer shook her head again.

Dumbfounded, Georgie began to grin nervously. "Wait a minute. You said you and what's her name . . ." she pointed to Sheila's photograph.

"Sheila."

". . . are lovers."

Jennifer nodded.

"You make love."

"Uh-huh." The scarlet hue of her cheeks darkened

as she grew defensive. "But we never called it anything."

"You're a lesbian and you don't even know it?"

"Passengers, we have begun our descent to the Des Moines municipal airport. Local time is twelve-thirty." The flight attendant's voice broke through Jennifer's reverie. "As we begin our final approach, please make sure that your seat backs and trays are in their upright and locked position."

Reluctantly, Jennifer relinquished the memory of that afternoon with Georgie. She had been so naive back then. Meeting Georgie had completely changed and opened up her life. They had become lovers, eventually. Nearly a full year later. But not until Jennifer had finally let go of Sheila. And that was one particular memory that Jennifer refused to think about now. Especially now.

Chapter 2

All thoughts evaporated as Jennifer leaned over to watch the patchwork ground reaching up to greet her. Roads crisscrossed perfectly, creating perfect little squares of land. She smiled as a familiar tug pulled at her heart. It had been too long, and an old homesick feeling settled in her stomach as the wheels of the airplane touched and then grabbed the runway.

A few minutes later, she was going through the walkway. Quickly scanning the faces in the crowd, her eyes instantly rested on her sister's smile. She grinned as she covered the few feet between them and pulled the shorter woman into a bear hug.

Jennifer stood back, each hand firmly clasped on her sister's shoulders, and surveyed Sally's features. Clear gray eyes smiled back at her.

"Sally, you're gorgeous. You haven't changed a bit."

"My hair's shorter." Sally had always worn her auburn hair long. Now it was cut shorter, bluntly reaching the top of her shoulders.

"Not as short as mine," Jennifer laughed, running her fingers through her own short locks.

Sally reached up and rubbed her sister's head. "Wow. That's short." She leaned back a little, taking it in, then nodded. "It looks good. *You* look good. Healthy."

"It's that Arizona sun. Hey, who's this?" Her eyes dropped down to rest on the face of a little girl peering up at her from behind Sally's leg. Jennifer squatted and reached out, ready to pull her niece into a hug. "Hi, Allison."

The little girl's eyes grew wide as she pulled away, hiding farther behind her mother's leg.

"Allison, you remember your Aunt Jenny."

Allison stared at her aunt, and Jennifer's heart sank a bit. Words eluded her.

Sally's hand went to her daughter's head, rubbing it gently. "Jenny is going to stay with us for a few days." Allison stood remotely still. "Let's go get your aunt's luggage, okay?"

Allison looked up at her mother and nodded. Jennifer stood, her eyes finding Sally's as they began walking through the terminal.

"Don't worry. She's shy like that with people she doesn't know. We won't be able to pry her away from you by the end of the weekend."

Jennifer nodded, trying to shrug it off. She knew her reaction was unreasonable, but she couldn't help it. *It's my fault she doesn't know me*, Jen thought. *I shouldn't have stayed away so long.*

They picked up her luggage and were across the parking lot and inside Sally's car minutes later. They made their way across town easily. Down Fleur Drive, up Grand Avenue, across 42nd Street. Nothing seemed to have changed since the last time Jen was there.

"You should see West Des Moines. You wouldn't believe all of the houses out there now. Jim and I are thinking about moving the kids out there next year." They drove through Drake University campus, then up through Beaverdale, where as kids they had spent hours riding their bicycles. Then they moved on down Urbandale Avenue.

"Where's the grade school?" Jennifer leaned forward, looking up at the familiar hilltop where she had spent her earliest years.

"Gone. They tore it down," Sally explained.

"No. How could they do that?"

Sally shrugged. "Who knows. It's been gone for years."

Feeling betrayed, Jen settled back in her seat. "Did they tear anything else down?"

"I don't think so," her sister laughed. "But they did knock down all the woods behind our old house. Remember that old barn with the hayloft that we used to play in? Gone. Nothing but new houses now."

Childhood memories were being crushed left and right. "Mom and Dad would shit," she muttered.

"She said a swear word, Mommy." Allison spoke up from the backseat for the first time.

"Oops." Unexpectedly chastised, Jennifer instantly apologized.

Sally chuckled in return. "I didn't realize how much I swore until Allison started pointing it out every time." She looked at Allison's reflection in the rearview mirror. "Right, honey?"

"Right, Mommy."

Sally waited until Allison seemed preoccupied again. She turned back to her sister. "She's going through a righteous stage," she grinned. "I'm not sure if that's good or bad."

"She'll grow out of it," Jen assured her.

"I sure hope so," Sally sighed. "It's not easy to be reprimanded by a six-year-old."

Within minutes, they were passing Merle Hay Mall and pulling into a short driveway. Sally's husband, Jim, was waiting for them when they arrived. He dropped a kiss on his sister-in-law's cheek and welcomed her with a big hug and an even bigger grin.

A little boy with a shock of fine white hair and the bluest eyes that Jen had ever seen was giggling with delight and tugging on his father's trousers.

With Allison's lukewarm response fresh in her mind, Jen was at first reluctant with her enthusiasm.

"Tommy?" His eyes met hers while his father hoisted him easily into his arms. He put a finger to his son's ribs and was rewarded with peals of laughter.

"Tommy? Can you say hi to your Aunt Jennifer?"

The little boy stopped squirming, wide eyes trained on the stranger before him. He placed one finger of his left hand securely in his mouth. He pointed another finger at Jennifer.

"Hi, Tommy."

The finger stayed where it was, inches from her face, while the little boy continued to search her features. He looked back to his father questioningly, his finger still hanging in the air.

"Say hi to Jennifer," his dad urged him.

Again the blue eyes turned to hers. "Ha," came the small voice, and Jennifer felt triumphant.

They all spent the next several hours settling in, catching up, and getting reacquainted. After several attempts to warm up to Allison, Jennifer decided to let well enough alone and not push it.

They shared an early dinner while going over the plans for the next few days. Several events had been planned for the reunion throughout the weekend. That evening was a casual gathering at Greendale Country club. Saturday afternoon a family picnic was scheduled, followed by a formal dinner in the evening. Another picnic was planned for Sunday afternoon for anyone still around.

As they went over the schedule, Jen thought ruefully that she hadn't planned for spending much time with her sister's family, and she told them as much.

"I could skip tonight's party, if you like. So we

can spend some time together," she suggested hopefully.

Sally slapped her leg. "Don't even think about it."

"Why don't you two go? I'll stay home with the kids," Jim suggested.

Jen's eyes lit up. "Perfect. Sally? Please come. I'm liable to drive around for hours trying to get my courage up if you don't go." She didn't have to twist her sister's arm, and within twenty minutes, they were in the car and on their way to the reunion.

Chapter 3

They arrived at the country club ten minutes later. Jen reluctantly stepped from the car and began to make her way down the path toward the clubhouse and botanical gardens.

"Oh god," Jennifer said. "Do we have to do this?"

Sally placed both hands on her younger sister's back and gave her a playful shove. "You can do it, kiddo. I can't believe you're this nervous."

"I can't either," Jen admitted. "In fact, I don't remember the last time I was this nervous."

"It's not like you."

"I know."

"You're always so confident."

Jen turned toward her sister. "You think so, huh?"

"Of course. I've always wanted to be more like you in that way."

Astonished, Jen glanced sideways to see if her sister was teasing. But Sally's face was earnest.

"I never knew that," she mused.

"Of course you didn't. It's not something one likes to admit to her little sister." They stopped walking as the clubhouse door loomed before them. A huge banner was draped above it. WELCOME GEORGE WASHINGTON — CLASS OF '77.

Jennifer groaned aloud. "I can't believe I let you talk me into this."

Sally rolled her eyes and tucked an arm through Jen's. "Come on. We'll have fun." She pushed the door open and the two of them stepped inside.

They found themselves in a long narrow hallway that led to a larger room, where picnic tables had been placed strategically along the perimeter. Dozens of people, indistinguishable to Jennifer's eyes, milled about, casually drinking and chatting in little groups.

"Hi!" A loud, singsongy voice greeted them. "And just who would you be?"

Jennifer's eyes fell to the perky, brown-haired woman who stood behind a picnic table immediately to their right.

"Hi." Jen found her voice.

"You know," the woman said in a puzzled voice, her eyes darting back and forth between the sisters. "I don't think I recognize either one of you. I'm Tina

Simms." She pointed to the round button pinned to her lapel. On the button was a black and white photograph, clearly from their high-school yearbook. Jennifer didn't think she'd ever seen this woman in her life.

"I'm —"

"Don't tell me," the woman shrieked abruptly, clearly excited about the role she was playing. "Show me!" She waved the two of them closer. "Find your button." Dramatically, her arm swept out to indicate the table before her. Nearly fifty of the round buttons were scattered across the table, each decorated with the yearbook photograph of a different graduate. Beneath each photo, someone had carefully lettered the graduate's name.

Jennifer slid a grimace at her sister before scanning the table for her name tag.

Her own face stared back at her from one corner. "That's me." Jen pointed to the button, and Tina eagerly swept it up, glancing at the photograph and then at Jennifer.

"Jenny Moreland?"

Jennifer cringed. No one had called her Jenny in years. Except her sister, of course.

Tina continued to glance back and forth between Jennifer and the picture. "I don't think I know you." Tina was clearly disappointed. "Wow," she said, handing the pin to Jennifer. "You sure look different."

Jennifer looked at the photo on the button and had to chuckle. "I sure do." The teenager smiling lazily up at her could have been anyone but the woman she'd turned into. Long, thick blond hair layered in a long shag framed softly pointed features.

Eyes thick with makeup were wide open. Innocent. She'd looked innocent. With a sigh, she fumbled to pin the button to her shirt.

"And who are you?" Tina turned to Sally.

"I'm her sister. I graduated a year earlier."

"Well, how nice of you to join us tonight. Have fun," Tina said smoothly, already turning her attention to a couple opening the door behind them.

Sally gently urged Jennifer away from the table. "Do you know her?" she whispered.

"Not a clue. Can we go home now?"

Exasperated, Sally punched her shoulder. "Knock it off, kiddo. You're stuck for at least an hour or two. Recognize anybody?" They had reached the main room of the clubhouse, and it took Jennifer several moments to realize that she was scanning the crowd without actually looking at anyone.

She shook her head. "They're bald. All of the guys are bald." Aghast, her eyes flew from one gleaming head to another. "They're twenty-eight years old, and they're all bald."

Sally laughed. "Don't you have any men in your life?"

"Of course I do. But the last time I saw any of these guys they had hair."

"We all change." Sally's voice sounded weary. "Come on, let's find a place to sit so I can get us some drinks. No hiding in a corner, now. I want you to mingle." She directed them to a table and tucked Jennifer safely on a bench before stepping away.

Jennifer sat quietly, trying to relax and shed her anxiety. She let her eyes wander about the room. She discovered that once she actually allowed herself to focus on each face, familiar features materialized and recognition soon followed.

She remembered these people. Some from as far back as kindergarten. Some were bigger than she remembered. Some smaller. Hairstyles were shorter, for both the men and the women.

"Jenny? Is that you?" Jennifer looked quickly to her right. A shorter woman with red hair and sparkling blue eyes smiled at her. Freckles covered every inch of her exposed skin.

"Lucy!" Jen jumped to her feet and threw her arms around the shorter woman. After a flurry of greetings and exclamations, Lucy joined her at the picnic table.

"You look great," Jen told her.

"So do you. You look so healthy. And I love your do."

Jen grimaced self-consciously and ran long fingers through her hair, wishing she hadn't had it cut quite so short. "A little radical for this group, perhaps."

"Fuck 'em," Lucy shrugged, tipping a bottle of beer to her lips.

Jen laughed. For a moment, Lucy reminded her of Georgie.

"What are you doing now? Where do you live?"

"Just north of Phoenix. I'm a pharmacist."

"A pharmacist?"

"Yeah," she shrugged.

"Good god. I'd have expected that you were doing something more exciting with yourself."

Jennifer shrugged again, fully prepared for this

common reaction. They spent the next few moments catching up, and Jennifer found herself searching for things to say.

"Have you seen anyone else here from the team?" The team was the George Washington Cherry Blossoms, better known as the girl's high-school basketball team. Jennifer had played all three years of high school. She'd been a forward, although she'd spent most of the time on the bench, while Lucy was the point guard.

"Sure. Tammy and Sandy are here. I saw Gina a few minutes ago. And Diane is here somewhere." Lucy's eyes scanned the crowd as she waved several women over to their table.

So Diane Miller is here, Jen mused. She felt slightly curious about the only known lesbian from high school.

Before long, Sally returned with drinks in hand, and a number of classmates began to gather at their table. Most of them had been members of the basketball team, and the majority had husbands in tow. She learned that several of the women had been married and divorced. Only two of the original teammates hadn't married at all. Jennifer was one. The other was Diane Miller.

Sally was thankfully deep in conversation with Lucy, giving Jen a chance to observe her former classmates. As she glanced around at the faces surrounding her, she thought how interesting it was that this particular group would gravitate together. Although she had spent quite a lot of time with these women when they were girls, she hadn't really felt particularly close to any of them.

But she hadn't really felt close to anyone back

then, she reasoned. Except for Sheila and Sally. No one else had seemed important to her. But surely someone here had held some special place in her heart? She shook her head, unable to remember, but suddenly desperate to find something from her past worth revisiting. Something other than Sheila.

Her eyes wandered outside the circle, moving from face to face as she identified some of the other classmates in the room. Her gaze rested on a young woman standing shyly away from the rest of the crowd. She was holding a glass tightly in one hand and watching the liquid that swirled inside with great interest. Occasionally she lifted her head, her dark eyes glancing around the room from beneath long, fine blond hair.

For the life of her, Jen couldn't place the woman. She looked vaguely familiar, but nothing in Jen's memory clicked. One thing was certain, however. The woman was terribly uncomfortable. *Even* more *uncomfortable than I am,* Jen thought.

Unable to drag her eyes away, she searched her memory. She wanted to come up with a name so that she could find a reason to talk to the woman. Heat rushed to her cheeks as familiar excitement fluttered in her stomach. Then Sally's elbow was digging into her side, demanding her attention. Reluctantly, her thoughts rejoined the group around her. Gina was telling a story about trying out for her college basketball team. Sally whispered something about Sheila before disappearing from her side.

In her peripheral vision, Jen could see Sally reaching for someone, pulling them close in a hug. Black hair. Shorter than she'd remembered. A familiar voice. Sheila.

Jen felt cold inside; her palms instantly went damp. The two were approaching, their voices growing clearer. She tried to focus on what Gina was saying.

"And then this girl takes the ball from me and looks me over, and then she said 'You're from Iowa, aren't you?' And I told her yes and asked her how she knew. Do you know what she said?" Gina looked from one face to another. "She said, 'Because you never step over the centerline and you never dribble the ball more than twice.'" A roar of laughter erupted from the table.

Jennifer could hear her sister calling her name, but she didn't want to look. She didn't want to talk to Sheila.

"Jen! Jenny! Look who I found!"

Groaning inwardly, she fixed a smile on her lips and turned in her seat to face her sister.

Sally was grinning broadly. "It's Sheila!"

Jennifer held her breath as her eyes swept over the woman standing beside her sister. Her body was fuller and heavier than before. The long black hair was cut short and poofed out in a way that made her look older. Green eyes peered out at her from behind heavy makeup. Bright red lips pouted ever so slightly.

Jen stood, uncertainly moved forward, and awkwardly held out her hand. Sheila's hand met hers, and their cheeks brushed in the stiff, formal way reserved for straight women who don't know each other.

Jennifer's bones chilled. If she'd had any doubt about how Sheila would react to seeing her, she had none now. Sheila was studying her carefully, her eyes flickering over Jen's features. One brow raised ever so slightly as her eyes focused on Jennifer's hairline.

"Sheila. How are you?" Jen was determined to get this over with quickly.

"Couldn't be happier. And you?" Her voice was clipped, with just a trace of a southern accent that Jennifer knew she hadn't had before.

"Better than ever," she replied, unable to break the stare between them.

From out of nowhere, an arm appeared around Sheila's waist, and a large, rough hand was thrust out in front of Jennifer. "Hey, Jenny."

"Hi, Bobby." With a sick feeling, she placed her hand in his and nearly gasped as he crushed her fingers. He was grinning at her, a knowing smirk on his features.

He knows.

With some satisfaction, Jennifer noted that Bobby seemed to be suffering the same fate as so many others of their male classmates. He was completely bald, and his belly protruded over his belt.

He pulled Sheila against him possessively while he chewed gum loudly, all the while staring at Jen with that unflinching smirk.

The silence grew uncomfortable. Sally stepped in and took control of the conversation.

"Where are you two living now?"

"We moved to Dallas about eight years ago," Bobby said.

With some relief, Jennifer tuned out the conversation and observed the couple quietly, looking for any sign or acknowledgment from Sheila.

"Do you have any kids?" Sally was asking.

Sheila rolled her eyes. "Three of 'em. All boys."

Jennifer felt her knees buckle. Sheila had children. Three boys. Jen felt betrayed all over again. It was easier not to know. It was easier just to imagine that Sheila had gone on without her. But she didn't want to hear about it.

"Hey, Bobby! Hey, Sheila!" Thankfully, they were interrupted by Gina, who waved them over to meet everyone. While introductions were being made, Sally threw a questioning look at Jen, who just shrugged and looked away, unable to meet her eyes.

"We were just talking about some of the crazy stuff we used to do," Gina was saying. "Like sneaking into the boys' locker room after practice."

"And cutting biology class," Lucy chimed in. "Nobody ever went to that class."

"Smoking in the rest room," somebody added.

"I never did any of that stuff." Sheila's voice boomed far louder than anyone else's.

For a moment, no one said anything. They all stared at Sheila. Jennifer was amazed. If anything, Sheila had been the ringleader whenever they were up to no good.

"Yeah. Right." Lucy's voice dripped with sarcasm. "You were a real angel, Sheila," she chuckled. "I seem to recall that it was you who always wanted to play spin the bottle. You who put Gina's bra in the freezer at one of my slumber parties. And weren't you the one who —"

Sheila's face grew red. "I don't remember doing anything like that," she insisted. "And if I did, it was because Jenny put me up to it. She always made me do stupid things that I didn't want to do."

Stunned by the vehemence of Sheila's words, Jennifer stared dumbfounded at the woman who had once been the most important person in her life.

The others in the group were also shocked, obviously surprised by what sounded like a completely unprovoked attack.

Finally, Lucy threw her head back and laughed. "If you say so, Sheila. But that sure ain't the way I remember it." She picked up a bottle of beer and tipped it to her lips.

"Jesus," Sally muttered under her breath near her sister's ear.

Jennifer turned to her sister and plastered a fake smile on her face. Through tightly clenched teeth she whispered, "Are we having fun yet?"

Sally gave her a wide-eyed, meaningful stare just as Jennifer felt an arm curling heavily around her shoulders.

Startled, she looked up into the face of Diane Miller, just inches from her own. Diane was smiling broadly.

"Hey, doll. You're looking hot," she said loudly. Too loudly.

Jennifer nearly choked as Diane's eyes slid over her boldly. Jen's memory of the once shy and gawky teenager was instantly blown away. The big-boned, hulking woman that towered over her was clearly self-confident, unbelievably handsome, and undoubtedly a bull dyke. And it was equally obvious that she didn't care who knew it.

Jen glanced at Sheila and Bobby, who were both barely hiding their distaste. As the desire to flee swelled inside her, Diane squeezed her shoulder and sent a playful wink her way. "Don't let her get to you, doll," Diane whispered, and Jennifer was somehow calmed.

A chorus of greetings erupted as Diane quickly became the center of attention. She greeted everyone smoothly before turning to Sheila. Deliberately and slowly, she looked Sheila up and down again before meeting her eyes and greeting her with a nod of her head.

"Sheila," she said simply, without acknowledging the husband who seemed to pull his wife even closer against him.

The tension was thick between them as Sheila muttered a greeting, her lips a careful straight line.

Warning bells were going off in Jennifer's mind. Something here was definitely not right. In high school, she and Diane had really no relationship at all except on the basketball court, and she couldn't recall Sheila ever even speaking to Diane. Why then, was Sheila glaring at the two of them? And why did Diane appear so triumphant, casually draping her arm around Jen's shoulder's and rocking back and forth on the heels of her boots?

Jen caught her sister's questioning gaze again and shrugged her shoulders, completely at a loss. "We were just talking about the good old days," Jennifer finally found her voice.

"Come on, were they really all that good?" Diane whispered and smiled at her hawkishly, making her squirm.

"Yeah," Lucy chimed in, "Sheila was just telling us what an angel she was back then."

Diane tipped her head back and laughed, her arm finally leaving its place around Jen's shoulders. "She was a real innocent, wasn't she?"

Had Jennifer missed something? Why was Lucy so antagonistic toward Sheila? And what did Diane know about Sheila? And about Jen, for that matter?

Thankfully, a small group of people that Jennifer barely recognized stepped between them, interrupting the exchange. Diane disappeared after throwing another wink, and Jennifer seized the opportunity to catch her sister's elbow.

"I think I've had enough excitement for one night. Let's go." She began to steer Sally away from the others.

"Wow. What was all that about?" Sally asked.

Jennifer shook her head. "I'm not sure. I think I only know about half of it." She tried to dismiss the speculation from her mind.

"Leaving so soon?" Tina Simms called out as they reached the door. Jen looked back quickly to reply, stopping short as she found herself face-to-face with the blond she'd watched earlier.

"Hi, Jenny," the girl said quietly.

Jennifer stared at the woman, frantically searching her memory. Surely she would remember a woman this gorgeous. Shy blue eyes gazed at her, uncertain. Waiting.

"You know me?" Stupidly, Jen grasped for conversation.

The other woman nodded, looking slightly wounded.

My god, she's gorgeous.

Jennifer searched for the giveaway name tag, but found none. She began slowly shaking her head, racking her brain. "I don't —"

The woman looked disappointed as she lifted a small hand to her brow and ran fingers through her hair. Shyly, she looked away.

"Heather?" Recognition slapped her. "Is that you?"

The small lips turned down for just a moment before spreading wide and lifting into a cautious smile. She nodded.

Jen fought an overwhelming desire to crush the smaller woman to her chest. Tongue-tied, she continued to stare.

"You're gorgeous," she blurted out, cringing as the words left her mouth.

"So are you." Heather returned the compliment, and Jennifer blushed.

"No, I mean really. You look fabulous." Jennifer continued to stare until Sally interrupted by holding out a hand in greeting.

"Hi. I'm Jennifer's sister, Sally," she said.

"Nice to meet you," Heather replied, taking Sally's hand and shaking it warmly.

Stammering, Jennifer looked back and forth between Heather and her sister. "We were just leaving."

Heather looked disappointed.

"Are you coming back tomorrow?" Jen asked quickly. "I mean, everyone's coming back to the park tomorrow, right?"

"I'll be here. Are you coming?"

"Yeah. We can catch up then, okay?"

"I'd like that," Heather smiled, and Jennifer nodded, nearly tripping over herself and then her sister as she opened the door behind them and pushed her way outside.

Chapter 4

"Unbelievable," Sally was saying as they retreated up the path toward the car. Night had fallen, and little lights lined the walkway to the parking lot.

"What is?" Jennifer was uncertain what Sally was referring to.

"The whole evening. I feel as if I've been through the wringer, and I was just watching the whole thing."

Jennifer didn't reply, thinking again about Sheila and Diane.

"What's the deal with this Heather woman? Is she

the one that you slept with?" Sally asked nonchalantly.

Jen stopped in her tracks. "No," she sputtered emphatically.

"Okay, okay. Relax," she began, then smiled mischievously. "I've just never seen you fall all over yourself in front of a woman like that before." She began to cackle loudly. "Is she your type?"

"Very funny." Embarrassed, Jen wrinkled her nose. "I was a stumbling idiot. Did you hear me? 'You're gorgeous. Do I know you?' " she mimicked her own words. "She must have thought I was a complete fool."

"You were kind of gushing," Sally admitted, her grin lopsided.

"Gushing?" Jen hurried along the path. Music and laughter from the clubhouse reached her ears.

Still laughing, Sally caught up with her. "Don't worry. You were fine. I'm sure she didn't notice you were —"

"— gushing," Jen finished the sentence for her.

Sally clamped her lips together to hide the smirk that threatened to escape. As she studied her younger sister, a thought occurred to her. "I just realized that I've never seen you with a girlfriend before. How come?"

Jen shrugged. "I guess nobody's been special enough to introduce to the family."

Sally considered this, then grinned at her sister. "Not even Diane Miller?"

Jennifer nearly choked. "I never slept with Diane Miller."

"She sure acted like you two knew each other awfully well. She's gay, isn't she?"

"Yes, she's lesbian. No, we never slept together. We weren't even good friends in high school."

"No?" They reached the car, where they paused for a moment before Sally climbed inside.

"No," Jen told her, then chuckled as she joined her sister in the car. "You're fishing, aren't you?"

"Maybe I am." Sally crossed her arms and leaned back in her seat. "How come you don't talk to me, Jenny? I miss that, you know. You're so far away. We never talk. I feel like I don't know anything about you."

Jennifer felt her throat constricting. "Come on, Sally. It's not like that. I'm just . . ." She let the sentence die.

"There's nothing you can't tell me, you know. You're my sister. I love you, no matter what."

"But you wouldn't understand."

"How do you know that?" Sally demanded. "What have I ever done to make you believe that?"

Jennifer considered this. "Nothing, I suppose. I guess it's just me."

"Then talk to me. Tell me about it."

"About what?"

"About what just happened back there, for starters. Why was Sheila such a bitch to you?"

"I'm not sure, really. I could guess, but . . ." She grimaced, remembering Sheila's words. *Jenny always made me do stupid things that I didn't want to do.*

"Does Sheila know you're gay?"

"I think so." Not a complete lie, she reasoned. Just not the whole truth.

Reading the hesitancy in Jennifer's tone, Sally started the engine, flipped the headlights on, and put the transmission in gear. "You didn't answer my original question." She changed the subject, trying to lighten the mood. "Is Heather your type, or what?"

Jennifer laughed. "You're relentless, Sally."

"I never get you alone for very long. I want to know what makes you tick."

Jennifer heard the underlying meaning of her sister's words. "Okay, okay." She threw up her hands as if to surrender. She settled back into the car seat, trying to remember Heather's features. "She was pretty hot, wasn't she?" Jennifer slid a look at her sister, trying to gauge her reaction.

Sally smiled. "I suppose she was."

Jennifer tilted her head to one side, trying to recall what was so attractive about the blond woman. "I can't quite put my finger on it. What's so attractive about her, I mean."

Sally wrinkled her nose. "She's striking. Is that blond hair real?"

Jennifer nodded. "It was shorter before. I think her mom permed it or something."

Sally shuddered at the thought.

"That's just the thing. She looked completely different when we were kids."

"Really? How?"

"I hate to say it, but she was kind of mousy. Her hair had that tight kind of curly perm, and she wore those big, thick glasses." Jen shook her head, unable to reconcile the Heather from high school with the Heather of today. "And braces. She had braces. Kids used to call her Tracks. And Four-Eyes."

"Tracks?"

"Railroad tracks. Braces. You know?"

Sally grimaced. "Kids are cruel. You didn't call her those names, did you?"

"No." An image of Danny Johnson crushing Heather's glasses beneath his foot came to mind.

"Oh my god." Jennifer said the words with such emotion that Sally stepped on the brakes, pulling over just inside the parking lot.

"What?"

Her mouth agape, Jennifer turned to her sister as the memory grew more vivid. "Do you remember when I got kicked out of school in sixth grade for fighting with Danny Johnson?"

"How could I forget? You were grounded for months."

"She was the one that Danny was picking on."

"Who?"

"Heather. He stepped on her glasses and smashed them." She shook her head, the memory clear now.

Sally looked confused. "I thought it was Sheila."

Jen's laugh was sarcastic. "Nobody ever teased Sheila." She shook her head again. "But Sheila sure was pissed at me for weeks about that fight." Thinking back, she remembered how she had agonized over Sheila's silence.

"How come I don't remember Heather? Were you guys friends?"

Jen had to think about it. "We didn't really run around in the same crowds or anything. But I always liked her. She was very sweet. Quiet. Very nice." Another memory of Heather in high school came to mind. "She used to come to our basketball games in high school, though. She even came to practice a lot. She was always sitting in the bleachers. She kind of stood out because nobody ever went to those games. And she always sat alone."

48

"That's sad. I hope Allison and Tommy never have to go through that."

"You don't have to worry. Your kids are gorgeous."

Sally threw an odd look at her sister. "Isn't that a sad commentary. You have to be gorgeous to get through school without other kids picking on you."

Jennifer watched her sister closely, for the first time wondering what it was like to be a mother. It couldn't be easy. It must be painful sometimes to watch your kids grow up.

She wondered if Sally endured as much pain as joy with Tommy and Allison. Sally had never really talked about it. *Or maybe she has and I just never listened,* Jennifer thought.

Chapter 5

A child was screaming, a high-pitched, shrill screech. Pots and pans, falling, crashing to the floor. Giggles. Louder than the screaming before. Clang, clang, clang. Too rhythmic to be unintentional. Loud voices. Her sister? A phone is ringing. Clang, clang, clang. Ring, ring, ring. Isn't someone going to answer that phone?

Silence. Something must be wrong. Breathing. Quick, shallow breaths.

Jennifer fought through the sleep that wouldn't let go. Slowly, she opened one eye and focused on the tip of one of the tiniest fingers she'd ever seen, just four inches from her nose and slowly getting closer.

She shifted her focus to the pair of huge blue eyes a short arm's length behind the finger. Tommy was standing beside the bed, fine blond hair tousled from sleep and a teddy bear held tightly under one arm.

"Jeffer." His voice was somewhere between silence and a whisper, as if trying out the sound for his ears only.

The finger was getting closer.

"Jeffer," he repeated, his tiny lips wrapping around the phrase experimentally.

Fingertip finally met nose. His gaze moving to the pair of sleepy eyes that peered back at him.

"Good morning, Tommy," Jennifer grinned and lifted her head.

"Jeffer."

"Jeffer? Do you mean Jennifer?"

"Jeffer."

"Do you know my name?" She reached out an arm and he moved against her instantly, dropping the teddy bear to the floor and climbing up on the bed. He grinned down at her and began to giggle.

"Jeffer."

Astounded and delighted all at once, Jen was instantly bonded to the little boy who was now crawling all over her and the bed, demanding with a pointing finger that she pick up the teddy bear that he had discarded just moments before.

"Knock-knock." Sally's face appeared in the doorway.

"He knows my name! He said it!" Was it ridiculous to be so excited that her nephew of nearly two years old was saying her name? She didn't care if it was.

"He did, I swear."

"I'm sure he did. Telephone." Sally was holding out the receiver and mouthing the name *Sheila.*

"Sheila?" Jen whispered.

Sally nodded, placing the phone in her sister's hand.

"Come on, Tommy. Let's go eat breakfast." Tommy scrambled down from the bed and placed one hand in his mother's.

"Jeffer." He pointed back at Jennifer and looked up at his mom.

"That's right, Tommy," Jen could hear Sally's voice as they padded from the room. "She's your Aunt Jennifer."

Still half asleep, she turned her attention to the phone. Why would Sheila be calling at this hour? Why would she be calling at all?

"Hello."

"Hey, sleepy head. Where did you sneak off to last night?" Her voice was quiet and casual, as if they talked to each other every morning on the phone.

"Home. We came home."

"We missed you. I missed you," she paused, apparently waiting for a reaction. But Jennifer was having trouble grasping any of the conversation.

"Do you have plans this morning? How about breakfast?" Sheila's voice made breakfast sound like an orgy.

"Breakfast?" Jennifer quickly came to her senses. "Just you, me, Bob, and the boys?"

Sheila clucked her tongue. "Actually, I had something a little more intimate in mind. Why don't you meet me at my hotel?"

Jennifer could feel her heart begin to race. How could it be that even now, a simple seductive innuendo from Sheila could make her heart do flip-flops?

"I don't think that's such a good idea," she managed to say.

"Jenny," her voice dropped down into hushed tones. "We need to talk. We don't have much time."

Jennifer felt what little resolve she had begin to crumble.

"I'm at the Savory," Sheila told her. "Room six-oh-two. As soon as you can."

"But —" Jennifer found her voice too late. A dial tone echoed in her ear. She lay back, staring at the ceiling. *How dare she even think about calling me. Like she's summoning me to her room!* She struggled to shake the sleep from her mind. "And I can't believe I'm even thinking of going," she admonished herself aloud.

Her thoughts began to race. Why did Sheila want to see her? Maybe she was being set up. Maybe she would walk into that hotel room and be confronted by Bobby. Confronted with what, she reasoned. That she slept with his wife when they were kids? It seemed unlikely.

Maybe Sheila just wanted to talk. Maybe she wanted to apologize.

Jennifer's imagination began to run wild.

Maybe she wanted to tell Jennifer what a mistake she'd made all those years ago. Maybe she wanted to leave Bobby. *Maybe she still wants me.* Maybe she just wants a fuck. Angrily, Jennifer kicked back the covers and swung her feet to the floor.

"I'm a masochist," she muttered. "I never should have come back."

She let memories of the passion they'd shared play in her mind. It had been so good with Sheila. Nothing and no one had captured her heart the way Sheila had. But no one had broken it the way Sheila had either, she reminded herself.

She thought back to the last argument they'd had. It was nearly ten years ago, on the evening before Sheila's wedding.

Finals were over less than one week before the wedding, and Jennifer returned to Des Moines still believing that the wedding would never take place. But it was impossible to get Sheila alone for even one minute. There were last minute plans to rearrange. The flowers weren't right; Sheila's gown was too tight; Jennifer's gown still had to be finished.

As the day drew near, Jennifer was an emotional wreck. Panic seized her as she tried desperately to capture just a few minutes alone. Sheila, for her part, seemed to know what was on Jennifer's mind. She avoided all of Jennifer's attempts at conversation until there was nearly no time left.

Jennifer gritted her teeth throughout the rehearsal and dinner on the night before the wedding. She sat stiffly and moodily, staring at Sheila, screaming in her mind. At last, Sheila's mother insisted that they take time out that evening just for the two of them.

"Come and stay at the house, Jenny. You've been away so long, and I know that you and Sheila have barely had a moment alone together. After all, you girls have always been so close. And it won't be the same anymore after tomorrow."

Their lovemaking that night was perhaps the gentlest ever. Wordlessly, they touched and caressed every inch of each other's bodies, tenderly committing every line and curve to memory. When at last they lay exhausted in each other's arms, Jennifer finally let all of the tears of frustration and hurt and anger slide from between her eyelids.

"Please don't marry him," she whispered hoarsely.

Sheila took her time replying. "I have to. I want to."

"But you *don't* have to." In the complete darkness of the room, she couldn't see Sheila's expression. "We can go away together. Just the two of us. You'd love Phoenix."

Jennifer could sense the other girl shaking her head.

"We can't do that."

"But we can." Hope rekindled as Jennifer prepared to play her trump card and finally say the words she'd practiced over and over. "I've met girls like us, Sheila. I have lots of lesbian friends who love each other the way we do."

"No."

Jennifer was completely taken off guard by the vehemence of Sheila's reaction.

"But we —"

"Don't say it." Sheila pushed herself away, putting at least an arm's length between them.

"But it's okay. We can be together, like other lesbians."

"I am not a lesbian." The words hissed out, slapping Jennifer like a physical blow.

Silence lay between them as Jennifer considered this. Confused, and yet somehow more certain, she crawled across the bed and sat down beside her friend.

"But I am, Sheila. I know that I am," she said quietly.

"Maybe you are, Jenny. But I'm not. And I don't want to hear about it. I don't want to know about that stuff."

Jennifer's heart sank. The realization that she was losing Sheila was finally sinking in.

"But what about us?"

"I don't know Jenny," she replied wearily. "I love you. You know that. I don't want anything to change. But we have to grow up."

The words angered Jen. "And growing up means that you have to marry Bobby Grimes," she said sarcastically. "I never should have gone away to college. I should have stayed here and —"

"And what? Nothing would be different. I still would have slept with Bobby."

Jennifer recoiled at her words. "You fucked him?"

Sheila groaned impatiently. "You are so naive, Jenny."

"Naive for believing in you, Sheila. I trusted you." Emotionally spent, she began to sob uncontrollably.

Sheila slid across the bed and gathered Jennifer in her arms. "I'm so sorry, Jenny."

"And I'm just stupid," Jen insisted when she found her breath. "I didn't think you'd go through with it. I thought you loved me."

"Sh. I do love you, Jenny. I'll always love you. I'll always want you." They held each other, whispering endearments and rocking each other until each gave in to exhaustion.

Emotionally shut down, Jennifer made it through the day of Sheila's wedding in a mindless fog. It wasn't until the vows were spoken and the rice thrown that she finally crumbled. And before Sheila returned from her honeymoon, Jennifer was back in Phoenix, where she moved in and took refuge in Georgie's arms.

Jen's teeth chattered, but she wasn't cold. After nearly ten years without speaking, what had Sheila's first words to her been the night before? She couldn't remember. She felt confused, her thoughts incoherent. But now here she was in Des Moines, and Sheila wanted to see her. What could she want? What could she possible say to make it more over than it already was? Jennifer didn't have the answer. But she knew she had to find out.

Jennifer stumbled to the bathroom, where she slowly and deliberately showered. *Meet me at my hotel.* The words played with her emotions. Sheila's voice had been so quiet, so seductive. She fantasized about their meeting until she had no doubt that they

"But we —"

"Don't say it." Sheila pushed herself away, putting at least an arm's length between them.

"But it's okay. We can be together, like other lesbians."

"I am not a lesbian." The words hissed out, slapping Jennifer like a physical blow.

Silence lay between them as Jennifer considered this. Confused, and yet somehow more certain, she crawled across the bed and sat down beside her friend.

"But I am, Sheila. I know that I am," she said quietly.

"Maybe you are, Jenny. But I'm not. And I don't want to hear about it. I don't want to know about that stuff."

Jennifer's heart sank. The realization that she was losing Sheila was finally sinking in.

"But what about us?"

"I don't know Jenny," she replied wearily. "I love you. You know that. I don't want anything to change. But we have to grow up."

The words angered Jen. "And growing up means that you have to marry Bobby Grimes," she said sarcastically. "I never should have gone away to college. I should have stayed here and —"

"And what? Nothing would be different. I still would have slept with Bobby."

Jennifer recoiled at her words. "You fucked him?"

Sheila groaned impatiently. "You are so naive, Jenny."

"Naive for believing in you, Sheila. I trusted you." Emotionally spent, she began to sob uncontrollably.

Chapter 6

Barely ten minutes later, she was rapping on the door of room six-oh-two. Then the door was open and there was Sheila, draped in an oversize button-down dress shirt. In one glance, Jennifer took in the shirttail that just reached Sheila's bare knees, and the naked calves and feet not far below. It didn't take a lot of imagination to guess what was — or wasn't — beneath that shirt. The curtains were drawn tight behind her so that Sheila's features were mostly hidden. But Jennifer didn't miss the lazy smile on Sheila's lips.

"I'm glad you came."

"You knew that I would."

"I hoped." Sheila reached out a hand to take Jen's, drawing her into the room before firmly closing and locking the door.

They faced each other, inches apart in the semi-darkness.

"You're taller than I remember." Sheila's head was bent back as she looked up into Jennifer's eyes.

Jennifer had no reply as she felt an odd sense of déjà vu envelop her. Standing so close, she could smell Sheila's hair and the soft, feminine smell of her skin. Vivid memories crashed into the present. Scents that she recognized, even after all this time. Ten years later, and it was still the same. Nothing had changed. Nothing mattered. Except Sheila.

"Why did you want to see me?" Jen focused on Sheila's lips, knowing how they would feel against hers. Already tasting them, feeling them on her body.

"You know why." Sheila stared into Jen's eyes, reading each thought, recognizing each play of emotion. She slid her hand up Jen's arm, above her elbow, beyond her shoulder.

Jennifer shuddered as she felt the cool flatness of Sheila's palm on the nape of her neck, urging her closer. She bent down, and time fell away as their mouths met with a fierce familiarity. Lips and tongues and bodies pressed into each other hungrily, greedily, in a long embrace.

"This is crazy." Jen's hands were on Sheila's shoulders, forcing their bodies apart. She stepped back, stumbling as she fought to keep her sanity.

Knees suddenly weak, she glanced around and fell back into the overstuffed chair behind her.

Her chest heaving, Jen looked up to see Sheila standing before her, her breath coming in quick, short gasps, her lips wet from the kiss they had shared.

Jen shook her head. "This is crazy," she repeated.

Sheila's bare feet covered the floor between them quickly, and she bent to put a soft finger to Jennifer's lips.

"Sh." She leaned over, replacing her finger with her own lips.

Jennifer turned her face away in lame protest.

"Sh," Sheila whispered again, lifting her head to stare directly into Jennifer's blue eyes. Without averting her gaze, she climbed onto Jennifer's lap, lifting the shirttail as she settled herself on Jen's thigh. The scent of Sheila's passion assaulted Jennifer, and she clenched her teeth against the recognition and against her own weakening resolve.

Their eyes did not waver as Sheila reached out to Jennifer's hands, slowly turning and lifting them until Jen's palms were on Sheila's breasts. Jennifer swallowed hard. They continued to stare into each other's eyes. No smiles now, just the thick, heavy curtain of seduction lay between them as their pulses quickened and their breathing shallowed.

Coherent thought left her as Jen allowed herself to weigh the luxury of Sheila's breasts in her hands. With immense pleasure, she let her thumbs and fingers trace over the puckering nipples as they hardened beneath the fabric of Sheila's shirt.

Sheila's lids began to droop. Jennifer felt a sense of satisfaction at knowing exactly what Sheila liked, exactly how to give her pleasure. Impatiently, Sheila ripped the shirt away, anxious for the feel of Jen's hands on her skin.

Sheila's whimper become a moan as Jen buried her face between the huge breasts, breathing deeply before pulling each nipple into her mouth. She was sucking hard, her tongue playing deftly as Sheila's moans grew louder.

As past and present blurred, Jennifer recalled how easily Sheila had been able to come this way, just from teasing her nipples alone. Jen eased back, her arms falling limp to her sides. Both women were breathing hard; passion clouded their eyes.

Jen's focus shifted to the damp heat of Sheila's crotch on her thigh, and she groaned aloud for the first time as she realized that her jeans were completely drenched and saturated with Sheila's passion.

Then, as if she could read Jen's thoughts, Sheila reached down, lifting her hips just enough to dip her fingers into her own wetness. She brought those same fingers to Jennifer's lips, where Jen felt intoxication engulf her as those fingers slipped inside of her mouth. She sucked deeply, drowning in the taste and smell of Sheila.

Sheila's tongue pushed into her mouth, and Jen felt her own dampness growing. Unable to hold back any more, she wrapped an arm around Sheila's waist, pulled her close, and plunged her fingers deep inside Sheila. Wild with pleasure, Sheila rocked against Jen's fingers, each thrust mirroring the force of their mouths and tongues against each other. At last Sheila called out, her body convulsing as she fell against Jen's chest.

"God, Jenny," Sheila began through deep breaths. "You're so good." Their mouths found each other again in a long, deep wet kiss. "Nobody's as good as you are," Sheila continued. "You still know my body like a book."

Through the fog of desire, Sheila's words seeped through. It occurred to Jennifer that after ten years Bobby should certainly know her body better than she.

"You've ruined me, you know." Sheila lifted her head and smiled teasingly. "Nobody else ever measures up to you."

Measure up? And what did she mean by *nobody*? Had Sheila had other lovers over the years? She was a married woman, after all. "Have you had all that many to compare me to?"

Sheila giggled nervously as she dropped her lashes. "Oh honey. There've been a few. But like I said, none of them were as good as you."

Torn between the demanding ache between her legs, and the sobering effect of Sheila's words, Jennifer was stunned. Her mind moved slowly. Was she supposed to feel flattered?

"Women?"

Distractedly, Sheila toyed with the collar of Jennifer's shirt. Conversation wasn't exactly what she had in mind. Particularly this conversation. "Of course women," she replied. "Why would I have an affair with a man? I already have one of those."

Jennifer's features closed off. She wasn't sure if she was sad or angry. But at a minimum, she was surprised. She'd never considered that Sheila might be with other women.

Sensing the change in Jennifer's mood, Sheila began trailing kisses along her neck while dropping one hand and seductively tracing the seam of Jen's jeans between her legs. When Jennifer stiffened, withdrawing from the other woman's touch, Sheila protested.

"Don't be jealous, Jenny," she pouted. "I never loved any of them. Just you."

Jennifer pulled back as far as she could. "You really slept with other women?" she asked, her incredulous tone giving away her contempt and disbelief all at once.

Sheila scowled, for the first time resembling the woman from the evening before. "I suppose you thought you were the only one."

"Well, yes. No," Jen replied slowly. "Actually, I never really thought about it." She withdrew even farther, and Sheila broke out of the circle of her arms, moving to her feet as she paced the room dramatically.

"What would you have had me do?" Sheila sulked. "You never returned any of my calls. And then we moved away." She stopped pacing, arms folded as she gazed down at Jennifer. "Why didn't you return my calls?"

Suddenly weary, Jen tried to find an answer. "I just couldn't."

Sheila's lips were a bitter straight line. "Was she your lover?" she asked quietly.

Jennifer's face twisted, not following the other woman's train of thought.

"The voice on the answering machine. The one that always answered the phone."

Georgie. "Yes." Jennifer's voice was unemotional. "No. Not at first. But eventually, yes."

Sheila grimaced as she sat on the edge of the bed. She hugged herself, suddenly far away. "I nearly went crazy when I couldn't reach you."

"You made your choice." Bitterness from all those years ago began to swell in Jen's chest.

"But I wasn't choosing him over you, exactly."

Jennifer couldn't harness the guffaw that escaped her lips. "That's not quite the way I remember it. You married him, remember."

"But I still wanted to be with you." Sheila's voice became shrill.

Jennifer tried to find her own anger but found only sadness and regret. She wanted to laugh, to rail against this woman who had caused her so much heartache, but she didn't have it in her.

"I did the right thing, Sheila. I couldn't share you like that. I wanted someone to love just me."

They were quiet for a few moments before Sheila broke the silence, her voice wistful. "I was such a stupid fool back then."

Jennifer couldn't deny it, and after a few moments, Sheila smiled at her cautiously. "Do you have a lover now?"

Surprised at the question, Jen shook her head. "No. Not now." Not for nearly two years.

"But you are still" — she hesitated — "with women?"

"I'm a lesbian, yes."

Sheila lifted a brow and cocked her head suggestively. "Well then," she began as she approached Jennifer and knelt before her. "Let me touch you, Jenny," she whispered, lifting a hand to trace the outline of Jen's breast. "Let me love you." She leaned over until their lips brushed. "Like before." She sucked Jennifer's lips greedily. "Like when we were kids."

A shudder of desire raked Jen's body at the very moment that Sheila's words twisted a knife in her chest. For the first time that morning, the old hurt began to swell, threatening to choke her.

"I should probably get going." She refused to let Sheila see her vulnerability. "I need to spend some time with my sister before the picnic this afternoon." She placed her hands on Sheila's shoulders and eased her away. She stared into Sheila's eyes, for the first time noticing the lines that creased their corners. Her own eyes grew misty. "Besides, I'm sure that Bobby will be returning soon."

Sheila dropped her eyes and looked around nervously without speaking. Jennifer watched her behavior quizzically as a sick foreboding washed over. Her gaze darted around the room, taking it all in for the first time. Her stomach lurched with dread as she fully expected Bobby to appear at any moment. Where was he hiding? In the closet? The bathroom? But no, she quickly realized, all was quiet. They were alone. But something else was amiss. Something that she couldn't quite put her finger on. Everything was too perfect. No suitcases, no clothing, no toiletries.

"You rented this room just for this." Even as she said the words, she couldn't believe it.

"So we could be alone," Sheila rushed in. "What did you expect? That I would invite you up to the room I was sharing with my husband and kids?" She mocked her. "We're staying at my folks' house. I rented the room just in case."

"Just in case," Jennifer cringed, internalizing the words. She had just had sex with a married woman. She suddenly felt dirty and sick to her stomach at the same time. She squirmed in the chair and stood up.

"I have to go." She headed for the door, but Sheila quickly stepped in her path.

"Please don't go, Jenny. We still have time."

"Until what? Until you have to meet your husband and kids?" She couldn't help the sarcasm that dipped into her voice. They stood face-to-face, each seething with unspoken words and frustration. "Bobby knows, doesn't he? I could tell by the way he was leering at me last night."

"I had to tell him." Sheila quickly licked her lips. "I broke down," she began haltingly, "after you moved. When I couldn't reach you."

"Is that why you were such a bitch last night?" she asked.

Sheila's face colored, her nostrils flaring. "Bobby threw a nutty when he found out. I didn't want to give him any ideas."

"I guess it's safe to assume that he doesn't know anything about the other women."

Sheila's face became pinched. "No. Nothing."

"Why don't you leave him, if that's what you want? If you're still attracted to women."

Clearly startled at the idea, Sheila looked as though it was the most ridiculous thing she had ever heard. "I would never leave Bobby. It's a good marriage, Jenny."

Jennifer's heart sank as she bit back a retort. Instead she nodded, trying to smile. "I'm sure it is," she managed. "But I do have to go now. My sister's waiting."

"You'll be at the reunion, though, right? Later this afternoon and tonight?"

Jennifer grinned a little, already dreading the rest of the day. "I imagine so."

"And perhaps you'll meet me here again? Later?"

Jennifer noted something near desperation in her voice, and she frowned, as confused as ever. She considered the shorter woman with mixed emotions. She wanted to say no, but she wasn't sure that she would be able to stay away.

"Perhaps," she finally sighed, before allowing herself the luxury of stepping into Sheila's arms once more. She breathed deeply, trying to commit to memory the smell of Sheila's hair and the way the curves of Sheila's body pressed against her own.

Chapter 7

Ten years earlier, Jennifer would have walked back into her sister's house without ever letting on that something had just happened between her and Sheila. After all, she had done it nearly every day for years. But now was different. She'd developed a conscience over the years. She felt guilty. And foolish. And completely duped. Besides, she didn't really think for a minute that Sally would believe that the wet spot on the thigh of her jeans was from spilled coffee.

Sheepishly, she sneaked back into the house, meeting Allison's reproachful eyes first.

"Hey, Allison. What's up?"

The little girl threw her a wide-eyed look and retreated quickly to the kitchen.

"Great," Jen mumbled, then took a deep breath and followed her niece to where she knew her sister would be waiting.

"Hi. Did you have fun?" Sally had just finished the breakfast dishes and was wiping her hands on a dish towel.

"Not exactly."

"Jeffer!" Tommy squealed with delight and left his blue-and-yellow dump truck on the floor in his haste to greet her. Jen scooped him up and gave him a quick hug. His unexpected display of affection threatened the already fragile grip she had on her emotions. She pulled out a chair and sat at the kitchen table. Tommy lasted all of ten seconds on her knee before squirming to get back to his truck.

"Where's Jim?"

"He's at the office."

"On Saturday?"

"Almost every Saturday."

Jen noted her sister's resigned shrug with a pang. Perhaps her sister's life wasn't as idyllic as she had thought. Allison had found her mother's leg, and was peering out at Jen with unblinking eyes.

"Don't change the subject." Sally's lips were pulled down in a frown. "What happened?"

Guilt, heartache, anger, and frustration all battled across Jen's features, each emotion struggling to dominate. She was cracking, nearly unable to contain herself. She glanced at Tommy, then at Allison, all too aware of the differences between herself and her sister. How could she be honest? And how could she have such a frank discussion in front of the kids?

As if reading her sister's thoughts, Sally placed a comforting hand on her daughter's head before suggesting that Allison go get her Barbie dolls. "You can play here on the floor with Tommy while I talk with your aunt." Allison nodded before bounding from the room.

"So spill it." Sally settled herself in a chair at the table.

Embarrassed beyond belief, Jennifer let the words slip out quietly. "She seduced me."

"What?" Clearly, the thought had never even occurred to Sally.

"It's not like I didn't know what she wanted." Angry with herself, she caught the look of shock on her sister's face and tried to backpedal. "Sheila and I were lovers. For years."

Allison wandered back into the kitchen, dolls in hand, and began to play on the floor beside them. Sally threw a cursory glance at her children before turning back to her sister.

"When?"

"From when we were about thirteen. Until" — she gauged her sister's reaction and cringed — "well, until the night before she got married."

"Holy shit."

"That's a bad word, Mommy." Allison reprimanded her without looking up.

"You're right, sweetheart. I'm sorry," she apologized absently. "Why didn't you ever tell me? My god, that's six years." She stopped and stared at her younger sister, mouth agape. "You were lovers all that time?"

Jennifer nodded. The difficult part was over. She'd said the words. Now she just had to fill in the details. So she started at the beginning, quietly telling the entire story, stopping only to answer one of Sally's many questions along the way.

"I was a complete fool," Jen sighed, coming to the end of the story.

"You were a kid," Sally countered.

"Actually, I was referring to this morning."

Sally's eyebrows lifted, and a smile touched her lips. "Well, okay, you might have something there," she agreed, her tone light as she shrugged her shoulders. "It is a little messy."

Jennifer appraised her sister. She'd expected something different. A reprimand, at the least. But Sally was smiling, a faraway look on her face as she returned Jen's gaze and chuckled softly.

"I know that you're in a fix right now, but I'm just so glad that you finally told me about you and Sheila. It explains so much."

"What do you mean?"

Sally took a deep breath, her eyes distant again. "I was so jealous of her when we were young. I always felt that she got between us. I know that's silly. But once she came along, I felt we weren't as close anymore."

Jennifer's heart sank. "Sally, I'm so sorry. I was running around with this huge secret that I didn't know what to do with."

"I know. But I didn't know that." Her eyes became wispy. "All I knew was that we weren't close anymore, and I blamed Sheila."

"God. I'm so sorry. I was such an idiot."

"You were in love. It's okay. I understand. Thanks for telling me about this."

Jennifer smiled, a rush of fondness for her sister tugging at her heart. "I'm sorry that I didn't tell you sooner. It would have made both of our lives a little easier, I think."

Sally nodded her head in agreement. "There's a lesson here, my dear."

"You're right. Absolutely. And I won't forget it."

"See that you don't," Sally teased her briefly before turning the conversation to her sister's current dilemma. "What are you going to do now? About Sheila, I mean."

Jen shook her head. "Absolutely nothing. Pretend nothing happened. Play it by ear. I don't know," she sighed. "Any ideas?"

Sally laughed. "None at all. What do you want to happen?"

Jennifer's eyes dropped as she frowned. "I'm not sure. I'm ashamed to admit it, but I don't know."

Sally regarded her sister carefully. "You can't still want her after all this time. She was an absolute bitch last night."

"I know. I know." Jen's cheeks grew crimson. "Believe me, I'm not proud about what happened this morning. I wish I could tell you that I don't feel anything for her. But I'm not sure."

"Jenny, she's married."

"I know." Jen lifted wounded eyes to her sister. "She has this hold on me," she shrugged. "I can't explain it."

Sally watched her sister carefully, her lips curved in a worried frown. "Whatever you decide to do, it's bound to be an interesting afternoon. Too bad I won't be there to see it."

Jennifer's eyes lit up. "Why don't you come? Bring the kids. It's a family picnic, isn't it?"

Sally smiled slowly. "Why not? For a couple of hours, maybe. But only if you're not going to complain about being there the entire time."

"I promise," Jen relented, hoping that maybe the afternoon wouldn't be so bad after all.

Chapter 8

Greendale Country Club was spilling over with people long before Jen and Sally arrived. A number of people hovered around a huge barbeque pit, where hot dogs and hamburgers sizzled over an open fire, and others were playing volleyball. Most were content just to socialize. A number of children were playing on swing sets, hanging on the jungle gym, or climbing on a variety of playground equipment.

Allison wanted to play in the huge sandbox, and so Sally and Jennifer found a picnic table in a nearby shady area and settled down. For the next hour, they filled up on hot dogs and Coke until they all had eaten more than enough. While Allison and Tommy played in the sand, Jennifer found herself chatting easily with many of her classmates that she'd met with the night before.

She spotted Sheila easily. Whether out of embarrassment, anger, or frustration, Jen decided to ignore her. She was aware that Bobby was nearby because she heard his loud voice often, but she saw no evidence of their three little boys in attendance.

The two sisters sat companionably, keeping an eye on both children and occasionally chatting with others who stopped by to greet them. Soon they noticed a little girl with dark brown hair standing beside Allison hesitantly, hands clasped behind her back as she smiled shyly.

"My name's Amy. Can I play with you?"

Jennifer watched as Allison lifted her eyes to consider the other girl.

"I'm building a castle." Allison spoke easily. "Wanna help?"

Amy grinned and threw a hopeful glance over her shoulder. Heather O'Brien stood some distance away, leaning against a large tree as she observed the little girls.

"Can I, Mommy?" Amy asked.

Jennifer looked from daughter to mother, her mind slowly taking in this new information. Heather was smiling and nodding her approval, and Amy didn't waste any time joining the other little girl in the pile of sand.

Jennifer's eyes floated back to Heather's, and her face blanched in an awkward smile.

"Would you like to join us?" Sally called, already

sliding along the pine bench to make room for the other woman.

"You wouldn't mind?"

"Of course not." Jen found her voice, her heart lifting as Heather shyly approached the table and sat down.

"You have a beautiful daughter," Sally said.

"Thank you. Are these your children?" She looked quickly from Sally to Jen. "Or yours?"

Jennifer shook her head emphatically.

"They're mine." Sally smiled.

"They're sweet. We've been watching for some time, and I couldn't keep Amy away any longer."

"I'm glad you came over. It's nice for Allison to have someone her own age to play with."

They watched the children playing together for a while, and Jennifer took the opportunity to observe Heather more closely. She looked so different from high school. Fine, long blond hair framed the delicate features of her face. A dash of light freckles covered fair skin across the bridge of her nose. Bright blue eyes, unhampered by eyeglasses, turned to Jennifer and smiled, crinkling at their corners.

"What about you. Do you have any kids?"

"No." Her face colored. "I don't think I do very well with them."

"Nonsense," Sally told her before turning to Heather. "She's just not used to having them around."

Sally and Heather began sharing anecdotes about their children, and after some time, Jennifer tuned them out. With one ear on their conversation, she let her eyes wander over the throngs of people milling about. She carefully gauged her own reaction as she

77

spotted Sheila, smiling broadly and laughing with — of all people — Diane Miller. Jennifer's jealousy leaped from nowhere, coming fully alive.

"Did your husband come with you?"

"I'm divorced," Heather was saying, her words seeping through Jennifer's consciousness and causing her head to snap around.

"You're single?" Too late, Jennifer realized that the enthusiasm in her voice was too eager and terribly inappropriate.

Sally's eyes narrowed at her younger sister, but Heather seemed not to notice.

"Yes, I'm single." She smiled as she reached out and touched the ring finger of Jen's left hand. "What about you?"

"Single. Very single," she smiled broadly, exposing perfect white teeth. The two women held each other's gaze a moment longer than necessary while Sally raised one fine eyebrow in amazement. Jennifer felt a faint tickling sensation in the pit of her stomach, and she quietly chided herself and the attraction she was feeling.

"Forgive me," Sally was saying. "But I don't know how you do it. I can't even imagine being a single parent."

"It's difficult," Heather admitted. "But I teach at the grade school that Amy goes to, so that makes it easier. It was much worse before she started school."

All three tired children joined them. Each girl crawled into her mother's lap, and Jennifer lifted Tommy in her arms.

"Do you still live in the area?" Sally asked.

"No. We live in Flagstaff now."

"Flagstaff?" Jennifer interrupted. "Really? I live in Phoenix."

Heather's jaw dropped. "No kidding?"

"Just north of Scottsdale, actually. I have a small ranch there."

"Really? I can't believe you're so close." The blue eyes that held Jennifer's were suddenly wide and childlike.

"Do you have any animals?" Amy's eyes resembled her mother's as they turned to Jennifer.

"A few," she nodded. "Cats. Dogs. Horses."

"Ooh! Mommy, I want to ride the horses. Can I?"

"Amy," her mother admonished. "That's not very polite."

"Would you like to?" Embarrassed, Jen knew she sounded too eager. "Maybe you two could come down some weekend. It's really not that far."

"I think we'd like that. Don't let me forget to give you my phone number."

"I'd like to go too." Allison's voice was a quiet whisper.

Jen regarded her niece closely, her heart hopeful. "You can visit any time you like, Allison. I'd love for you to see Arizona. It's beautiful there."

Allison turned to look up at her mother. "Can we, Mommy?"

"Yes, Allison. We will."

"Promise?"

"I promise." Sally hugged her daughter tightly and dropped a kiss on the top of her head while her eyes met Jennifer's with quiet triumph. After a moment, Sally turned her attention back to Heather. "What do you think of the reunion so far?"

Heather considered the question thoughtfully. "I'm reserving judgment until the weekend's over," her tone wasn't encouraging.

Jennifer threw her sister an I-told-you-so stare. "See? I'm not the only one who has misgivings about being here."

"I can't believe you guys." Sally raised an indignant chin. "I had a wonderful time at my reunion." She proceeded to recount one highlight after another with much enthusiasm, then concluded by saying, "It was a fabulous weekend. I can't wait for the next one." Then she grinned naughtily. "Do you remember David Simmons?"

Jennifer searched her memory until the face that matched the name came to mind. "Tall and gangly? Black hair with freckles."

Sally nodded. "I had the biggest crush on him all through high school. He was at the reunion and he actually came over to me and told me that he'd had a crush on me back in school. Can you believe it?"

"That is so sweet," Heather smiled.

"What made him tell you?"

"He said that he'd always wanted to tell me and that he knew he'd kick himself for another ten years if he didn't get up the courage that night."

Jennifer began to tease her sister, watching Sally blush as she talked about David. They spent the better part of an hour talking, continuing their conversation about reunions before moving on to the topic of kids and parenthood. Heather and Sally slipped into an easy conversation, sharing secrets and lamenting how quickly the kids were growing.

Jennifer settled back and listened as they chatted, content to add an occasional comment while she watched each woman grow more animated. She watched Heather closely, recalling memories of Heather as a child. She had been so painfully shy. So introverted. Thinking back now, Jen could barely recall any conversation that they'd shared.

Her most vivid memories of Heather were of her sitting in the bleachers while the girls practiced basketball. Jen remembered that throughout their senior year, when Sheila had been so absorbed in popularity and boys, Jen could look up into the bleachers at every practice and see Heather sitting there, arms wrapped tightly around her knees as she watched them play. In those days, Jen had used basketball as a means to eat up the time that she was used to spending with Sheila. Each day after practice, she would climb those bleachers and settle a few rows away from Heather. Their conversation was quiet; it was mostly about basketball and about teachers. Jennifer was far from the best on the team, but Heather always encouraged her to do better, pointing out subtle ways in which she could improve.

Heather knew the ins and outs of basketball far better than most of the girls on the team. She had explained that she'd spent countless hours in the driveway with her father while he drilled the fundamentals into her head. When Jennifer told her that maybe she should go out for the team, Heather had only laughed nervously. "I'm better at watching than playing," she'd said as she tapped the pine beside her.

Before long, a number of people had gravitated to

their table. Children were suddenly everywhere, laughing and playing. One introduction after another was made, until Jen's mind was spinning with names and faces from both past and present.

She wasn't a bit surprised by the reaction of classmate after classmate as each realized exactly who Heather was. Nobody could believe what a transformation she'd been through, and Jennifer found herself cringing at the callous remarks that many made.

Through all of the comments, Heather remained poised, smiling graciously at every compliment. Jennifer, for her part, couldn't help the desire to protect Heather from their stares and insensitive words. She caught herself thinking that she'd always felt that way about Heather. That she'd wanted to protect her somehow even back in school, when everyone was making fun of her. *But we're not kids anymore*, she told herself, and Heather seemed to be taking it all just fine.

Lucy and Gina approached the table a few moments later, insisting that they needed more players for a softball game. After much ribbing, Jennifer gave in and took the leather glove that Lucy thrust in her lap.

"Come on, Heather. What about you?" Lucy grinned.

Heather shook her head. "Not me. You guys go ahead. I'll watch."

Reluctantly, Jen stood and looked down at Heather, a slow smile touching her lips. "Just like old times, eh?"

Heather's chin tipped up and she laughed. "Just like old times."

Feeling triumphant that Heather recognized the small secret they shared, Jennifer didn't miss the wide grin on her sister's face before she turned and strode toward the ball field with Lucy and Gina at her side.

Chapter 9

A large group made up of mostly men and some women were dividing themselves into separate teams. Jen allowed herself to be shuffled back and forth until they finally settled it. She was to play along with Diane, Gina, and a group of eight men, while Lucy joined the opposing team, which included Sheila's husband, Bobby.

Sheila must be nearby, Jen mused, but she refused to look for her. She regretted her decision to join in the game. She hadn't touched a softball since she was about twelve years old.

They assigned her to play second base, and after a quick toss of a coin, she headed out to her position. She sensed Diane beside her as she walked.

"I don't suppose you have anything to do with that shit-eating grin plastered all over Sheila's face today."

Stone-faced, Jennifer glanced at the taller woman. "What do you mean?"

"Look." Diane stopped short, touching Jen's shoulder lightly before slipping a pair of sunglasses from her nose and folding them slowly. "Don't take this the wrong way. I don't know what's going on now, but I do know what went on before." She frowned and tapped the sunglasses against the palm of one hand before placing them in the breast pocket of her shirt. "I think we should probably talk later. There are some things you probably should know."

"Like what?"

"I'll explain later. When there aren't so many people around. Just be careful, okay?" She threw out the last words ominously before slipping a large leather mitt over her left hand and jogging out to right field.

Jennifer set her jaw and took up her position at second base. A chill swept over her, and she shuddered. She wasn't sure what Diane was alluding to, but she could guess. And she didn't like the road her mind was taking. *Christ. I haven't had this much drama in my life since I lived here,* she thought ironically.

She'd managed to ignore Sheila's voice and avoid her gaze since they'd arrived. Now she let her eyes wander over the crowd of spectators behind the backstop. Sheila was easy to spot. She sat in the second row and directed a lazy, knowing smile Jennifer's way.

Uneasy, Jen looked for Bobby in the opposing team's dugout. Relief washed over her as she saw that he was oblivious to his wife's attention as he slapped a friend's back and guzzled a can of beer.

Moments later, the first batter stepped into the box, and Jennifer's mind and body slipped automatically into game mode. *Funny how it all comes back so easily*, she found herself thinking.

Three outs later, she trotted off the field, thankful that she had survived the first inning without touching the ball once. She glanced toward the picnic table where she'd left Heather and her sister, panic rising as she discovered that the table was empty. Her eyes scanned the crowded bleachers and quickly found Heather, just on the other side of the fence, smiling and waving her over.

Jennifer stepped over to the fence, her fingers curling through the links automatically.

"Where's Sally?"

"I hope you don't mind. She thought it was time to get the kids home, and I offered to give you a ride later. Is that okay?" A shy, hopeful smile reached her eyes.

"Of course. You don't mind?"

"Not at all."

She silently thanked her sister and wished that she'd never agreed to participate in the softball game. They continued to stare at each other awkwardly, the familiar giddiness pulling at Jennifer's belly as she searched for something to say.

"What about Amy?"

"She went with your sister. I couldn't drag her away from Allison."

Jennifer nodded, tongue-tied. Her already ragged emotions were working overtime. Surely the feelings she was having were terribly misplaced.

She felt a hand curling about her waist at the same moment that Sheila's perfume reached her nose.

"Hey, sweetie." Sheila's voice was deeper than normal.

Both women watched Jen. A small frown was on Heather's lips, and a leering grin was on Sheila's. Stammering, Jen tried to introduce them. Heather nodded coldly while Sheila insisted that she didn't remember who Heather was.

Jennifer grew visibly nervous and avoided both of their glances. Someone reminded her that she was batting next. As she bent to pick up a bat, she felt Bobby Grimes's stare on the back of her head. Sure enough, when she glanced down the first base line, his eyes met hers. He looked like he was seething.

She struck out. She wasn't sure whether she was disappointed or glad as she grabbed her glove and trotted back onto the field.

Her stomach knotted when Bobby stepped up to the plate, the first batter of the inning. Slamming her fist into the palm of her glove, she hoped fervently that he would strike out. Or fly out. Or hit a home run. Anything so that she wouldn't have to touch the ball.

"Strike one!"

Two more.

"Strike two!"

Hope soared. *Just one more. One more.*

With a loud crack, the bat swung around and met the ball soundly. Jen watched the ball sail high to her left, soaring over Diane Miller's head and dropping near the fence.

Bobby ran hard as the crowd cheered and Diane raced for the ball. He rounded first base as Diane scooped up the ball, and Jennifer found second base with one toe and braced herself for Diane's throw. A quick sideways glace told her that Bobby was digging in, eyes wild as he ran right at her.

Tag him. I have to tag him. With a thud, the ball snuggled into her glove. In a single motion, her arm swept down as she adjusted her position, facing him squarely. Too late, she realized he wasn't going to try avoiding the tag. He was barreling down on her, sliding. *Sliding.* Legs thrust in the air, booted feet slamming into her legs as his elbow sent a jolt to her forehead.

She felt herself flying backward, falling until her back slammed against the ground and the air was forced from her lungs.

Quiet. Darkness. She was floating. Images flickered in her mind. Buzzing sounded in her ears. Voices. Suddenly loud and angry. She opened her eyes and blinked hard to shield the sunlight. She was thankful when a shadow fell across her, shading her from the bright light.

"Jenny? Are you okay?" Concern. She recognized the voice. Vaguely. She blinked again. An angel's face hovered just above hers.

No. Not an angel. "Heather?"

Relief washed over Heather's face. "Are you okay? Can you move?"

Jennifer tried lifting her head. A shock of pain split her skull as she became aware of the people and sounds that surrounded her. Wincing, she let Heather help her to sit up as she recognized Diane Miller's growl just a few feet away.

"What did you think you were doing?" Diane's face was inches from Bobby's. "This is a game, asshole. A game." She thumped a pointed finger into his chest and pushed him away before turning and squatting beside Heather.

"You okay? Everything working?"

"I think so," Jen managed to whisper. By then, the bleachers had emptied, and Jen was surrounded by her old friends. Lucy was on her knees, inspecting the growing welt on Jen's forehead and calling for someone to bring some ice.

Jen insisted she was fine and convinced them to help her stand. They walked her out of the ballpark and found a shady area beneath several large trees where she insisted that she sit down and take a quick inventory. She rejected suggestions that she go to the hospital, politely telling everyone to go back to the game and that she would be all right.

Heather sat quietly beside her as Jen closed her eyes and willed the pain in her head to go away.

"Your knee looks pretty torn up," Heather said quietly. "I have a first-aid kit in my car. Will you be okay while I get it?"

Jennifer mumbled that she would be fine. When all was quiet a few moments later, Jen peered out from beneath heavy lids to see Heather still sitting beside her. Embarrassed, she tried to smile.

"Really. I'll be okay."

Heather seemed to hesitate, a frown pulling her eyebrows together. "I'm not sure if I should go just now. I think someone wants to talk to you."

Jennifer managed to glance in the direction of Heather's tilted head. Sheila stood some twenty yards away, hands on hips and her lips a straight line as she stared back at Jennifer. Oddly, Diane was standing just inches in front of the other woman, her head bobbing as she spoke to Sheila in hushed tones.

Jen watched as Sheila tried to sidestep Diane, only to find the taller woman blocking her path once again.

Jennifer groaned, willing Sheila to turn away, not wanting another confrontation today. Not wanting another confrontation ever. She closed her eyes and leaned her head back against the trunk of the tree. After several moments, she heard a soft sigh from Heather and lifted one eyelid enough to see that Diane had managed to steer Sheila away. Diane took a seat on the end of the bench as Sheila climbed back into the bleachers.

"What a mess," Jen muttered.

Heather looked at her questioningly before standing and brushing grass from her shorts. "I'll go get some ice and that first-aid kit now."

Chapter 10

Heather returned shortly, a bag of ice in one hand and a familiar red, white, and blue first-aid kit in the other. Jen accepted the ice pack, placing it against her brow as they bent to inspect her knee.

"Looks like you lost some skin."

"He got me good," Jen agreed as she looked over the area. "I can't remember the last time I got scraped up like this. Probably when I was ten years old."

"Amy gets scratches and scrapes all the time," Heather said. She pushed aside Jen's protests and began to gingerly clean and dress the wound. She spoke quietly about her daughter while she worked. "It's funny," she concluded, carefully covering Jen's knee with a large Band-Aid. "Years ago I couldn't imagine myself as a mother. Now I can't imagine myself as anything else." Her task complete, she uncurled her legs and stretched out on the grass beside Jen.

"She's a sweet girl. You must be proud of her."

Heather's smile was soft. "I am," she admitted. "It hasn't always been easy for her. But we've done all right. She's happy."

Jen studied her carefully, uncertain whether to pursue the topic. "Does her dad live nearby?"

Heather shook her head. "She doesn't really remember him." She hesitated, biting her lower lip as she assessed the other woman. "I met Amy's father while I was going to school out east. By then the braces had come off. I'd gotten contact lenses and had let my hair grow straight." She lowered her eyes and began absently running her fingers through the grass. "John was the first guy to pay attention to me, and I was overwhelmed by it. I got pregnant. We got married . . ." Her voice trailed off.

Heather grew quiet. Jen watched her closely, captivated, her heart heavy with the pain that she knew the memories must be stirring.

"How long were you married?"

"Only about a year and a half." Heather's smile was ironic. "I think he's somewhere in Florida."

Jen searched her eyes, looking for clues. "He didn't hurt you, did he?"

"No," came the quick reply. "If anything, it was the other way around. I didn't love him."

"I'm sorry," Jen said, knowing the words were inadequate.

They continued talking for some time. Heather explained how she and Amy had moved to Flagstaff where Heather eventually earned her teaching degree. In turn, Jennifer told Heather about her life in Phoenix. Occasionally, they glanced over at the softball game before turning back to their conversation.

The throbbing in Jennifer's head began to subside, and she lowered the ice pack for Heather's inspection.

"Ooh," Heather grimaced. "That's quite a shiner you've got there."

Jen wrinkled her nose and felt the swollen lump. Thinking of Bobby, and then Sheila, she spoke aloud. "I knew I'd regret coming back here."

A small line creased Heather's brow. "I hope you don't regret *everything* about coming back."

Abashed, Jen smiled. "No. Not everything."

"Your sister seems glad to have you here. She's very nice. I like her."

"She is, isn't she?" Jen grew thoughtful and blinked hard, trying to arrange her thoughts. "I'm beginning to realize that I've kind of isolated myself from her a bit." She stared meaningfully as she considered this. "My fault. But I've missed her, and it's been good to see her."

Heather nodded, seeming to understand. "Well, for what it's worth, I'm glad you came back."

Jen blushed, embarrassed. "I'm glad you're here too." She was quiet for a moment. "What made you decide to come back?"

"Interesting question. Why do you ask?"

Jen glanced over to the softball field. "I don't know. I just imagine that everyone has one reason or another. Mostly I think to see how their lives stack up against everyone else's."

"What about you? What's your reason?"

"I asked you first."

"Fair enough." Heather sighed, choosing her words carefully. "To exorcise some old ghosts." Her eyes lifted shyly. "I'm not sure how well you remember me back in school. Most of the kids teased me quite a bit."

Jennifer felt herself wincing. "I remember."

Heather nodded and lifted a hand, sliding her fingers over the top of her head and shaking back long blond hair. "I think I came back to face some things that I wasn't able to face when I was a kid. I wanted to see if people had changed. If they would treat me differently."

"And they have."

Heather nodded again. "But I'm not sure if they're treating me differently because we're older, or if it's just because I'm not an ugly duckling anymore. In either case, I wanted to show up just to say fuck you without actually saying the words."

Jennifer laughed.

Heather shrugged. "Closure. That's what I'm looking for." She looked back at Jen and tipped her head. "What about you?"

"*Closure* is a good word." Jen grew uncomfortable, not knowing what, or how much, to say. She glanced over at the ball field again, unable to meet Heather's steady gaze. "The past haunts me sometimes. I think I was hoping to finally put it all behind me." Her eyes touched Heather's briefly. She grew embarrassed, wanting to say more, to better explain. Heather watched her steadily, silently urging her to continue. "I'm still trying to let it all go," Jen finally sighed.

A reassuring smile crinkled Heather's eyes. "That sounds familiar," she said softly. "I'm discovering that letting go isn't as easy as I'd hoped."

"Ha. You too?" Jen's voice held a note of bitterness.

Heather pulled her knees up, wrapping her arms around her legs as her chin rested on one knee. "The question is," she began, her voice almost teasing, "do you want to let go?"

Jennifer sobered, her eyes finding Sheila's features as she sat in the stands, calling out encouragement to her husband. Images from that very morning floated to her mind. *Fool. Fool. Fool.* She shook her head as if to toss the memory aside. Heather was watching her, a serious frown pulling at the corner of her lips.

"It's gotten a bit more complicated," she began slowly. "But yes, I really do," she finished with certainty.

"Then I hope you can."

A chorus of cheers rose from the ball field, and their attention was drawn to the game as Bobby rounded second base and headed for third. Sheila was on her feet, calling out to her husband along with the other spectators. Bobby stepped on third base and then on to home plate before the ball even reached the infield.

As Jennifer watched the scene, she knew without looking that Sheila's eyes were on her again. When she allowed herself to look toward the stands, Sheila's smug expression greeted her. Heather took it all in, her eyes floating back and forth between the two women.

"Sheila." Heather spoke the name aloud, and Jen found her attention swinging back to the woman beside her.

"Excuse me?"

"She's who you want to let go of." Her face colored lightly as she stared back at Jen's slack jaw. "I suppose it's none of my business. But I'm right, aren't I?"

Jen stared at Heather incredulously before her face broke out in a grin. She began laughing at herself. The laughter continued until the pounding in her head reminded her of the headache that had only just begun to pass. Wincing, she gathered herself and leaned back against the tree once more.

"I must be the most incredibly naive person here." She spoke to the branches of the tree before turning her attention back to Heather. "Does everyone here know about me and Sheila?"

Now it was Heather's turn to grow embarrassed as she shifted uneasily. "Pretty much," she shrugged. "If they were paying any attention."

Jennifer's jaw clenched as relief and anxiety battled. Relief finally won out. There was no need to pretend. "And you were paying attention?"

A smile crept onto Heather's lips. "I was." She hugged her knees to her chest. "Maybe you've forgotten. But we talked nearly every day in high school."

"After practice. Of course I remember."

"You were obsessed with her."

Jen's eyes narrowed at this information. "Was I?"

The blond head nodded. "I'm sorry, I shouldn't —"

"No. Please. This is good for me to hear. My memory about some things is kind of clouded." She battled the confusion she was feeling.

"I only found out last night that Sheila had married Bobby. Did you know?"

An image from Sheila's wedding flashed in Jen's mind, and the absurdity of the whole story struck her. "I was her maid of honor." She nearly giggled.

Heather's jaw dropped. "No. How could you?"

"I don't know." Jennifer shook her head. "Crazy, huh? It's a long story."

Heather regarded her closely. "And it's a short weekend."

Jen laughed. "Remind me to tell you about it when you and Amy come down to visit." She said the words even though she didn't believe for a moment that it would ever happen.

"I will." Heather wrinkled her nose and stretched out her legs. "We should probably be going. It's getting late."

Jennifer agreed that it was, and slowly unwound her stiff body to stand. They walked toward the parking lot slowly and companionably, continuing their conversation as they went. It didn't occur to Jennifer that she should turn back and say good-bye to the others.

The drive back to Sally's house was short. As they rounded the corner of her sister's street, Jen found herself groping for something to say, something to solidify the closeness she was feeling.

"Thanks for fixing me up. And for the conversation," she said awkwardly. "I enjoyed it."

"Actually, I'm the one who needs to thank you," Heather replied.

"For what?" Jen pointed out her sister's house.

"For being so nice to me back in school." Heather's face grew hot as she pulled into the driveway. "For kicking the shit out of Danny Johnson back in grade school. For not calling me Tracks. For talking with me every day after practice." She turned off the car's engine but continued to stare straight ahead through the windshield.

Each word caused Jennifer's heart to constrict a little more. She turned to face Heather, who continued to avert her eyes, her jaw clenching.

"You don't have to thank me." Jen reached out, lightly touching Heather's elbow.

"Yes, I do." Heather's blue eyes were bright as they met hers. "It's one of the reasons I came back. Closure, remember? I was hoping that you would be here. I wanted a chance to tell you that you made a difference in my life. You were my friend. So thank you."

Jennifer searched the other woman's eyes, trying to think back and remember what impact they might have had on each other's life. Day after day they had sat together on those bleachers. Day after day Jen had poured her heartaches out. But Heather had never spoken of her own. The realization came to Jennifer suddenly, and she felt ashamed.

"I didn't do anything special." She realized she still held Heather's elbow, and she dropped her hand to her side.

"But that's the point. You were just you." Heather seemed to gather herself, gaining confidence. "And while I'm on a roll, I may as well take a hint from your sister and admit that I had the most incredible crush on you all through high school." Her grin was wide and lopsided. "And I hated Sheila Hoyt."

"Really?" Suddenly euphoric, Jen felt a silly smile emerge on her lips.

"Really." Heather rolled her eyes. "And I can't believe I'm telling you this." She reached for the door handle. "Come on. My daughter's waiting."

"But this is just getting good," Jen pouted, her voice teasing.

Heather raised one slim eyebrow. "Sure. Your body may be bruised, but your ego's doing just fine, right?"

Suddenly enjoying herself, Jennifer raised an eyebrow of her own and couldn't control the grin that tugged at her lips.

Chapter 11

With Heather's help, Jen spent the next twenty minutes trying to explain to Sally just how she had received all the bruises and lacerations in the few hours they had been apart.

It wasn't until after Heather and Amy had left that Sally followed her younger sister into her borrowed bedroom and began asking questions.

"Do you think he did it on purpose?"

"I don't know." The events of the day had begun to catch up with Jen, and it reflected on her features. She looked tired as she ran a hand through her hair and sighed. "Probably," she conceded. "He could have avoided me if he'd wanted to."

Sally tucked her bottom lip between her teeth as she considered her sister. "Do you suppose he knows about this morning?"

Jennifer winced as she settled down on the bed. "Maybe. I don't know. Why would Sheila tell him?"

"Why would she have invited you to that hotel room in the first place?" Sally countered. "She's up to something. I don't trust her for a minute."

"You're probably right." Jen closed her eyes briefly. "I can't believe I was so stupid this morning. Big mistake."

A hint of an amused smile touched Sally's lips. "I'm glad to see you're coming to your senses, at least."

"Better late than never?"

"Something like that." Sally crossed her arms and settled down on the bed beside her sister, concern resurfacing on her features. "Maybe you shouldn't go tonight. You're probably walking into trouble."

"What? And miss the reunion?" She mocked. "Never."

Sally slapped her sister's leg playfully. "Very funny. But seriously, maybe you'd be better off not going. It may not be safe."

Jennifer considered the idea, liking it for a brief moment. But a slow smile curved on her lips as she thought of Heather, and she dismissed the idea.

"What's that grin all about?" Sally didn't miss much.

"Heather."

"I thought something might be going on."

Jen's grin widened. "She told me that she had a crush on me back in high school."

"Really?" Sally's enthusiasm was genuine.

"Thanks to you and your David Simmons story."

"Glad I could help." She tipped an imaginary hat before lifting an inquiring brow. "Is she a lesbian, then?"

Jen's smile faded. "I don't know. I guess I just assumed she is. I'm probably getting my hopes up for nothing."

"I don't know. I think she seemed more than casually interested in you."

"You think?" She let her thoughts drift, until she realized that she would be disappointed if Heather turned out to be straight.

"She seems nice," Sally was saying.

"She is. She always was. Even when we were kids and everyone made fun of her. I never saw her get mad."

"She could have become very bitter."

Jennifer nodded. "But she's not. She's still quiet. Not as shy as before, just understated. And she's developed quite a sense of humor."

"Maybe you two will work something out. Flagstaff isn't that far away."

"I don't want to get my hopes up too much."

Sally tapped her sister's leg again. "Take a risk, silly. The weekend's almost over."

"I can't believe I'm going home tomorrow. I just got here." She turned sad eyes to Sally. "I'll stay longer next time, I promise. May I come back for Christmas?"

"I've only invited you every year for the last eight years. Of course you can come."

"I'll be here. Did you notice that Allison actually spoke to me today?" Her smile was hopeful.

"I told you she'd come around."

Feeling an unreasonable sense of accomplishment, Jen yawned. "I think I'll lie down for a while before I have to get ready for tonight."

"Good idea." But before Jennifer could leave the room, Sally steered the conversation to the topic of what Jennifer would wear to the formal event that evening, insisting that she borrow a dress. But Jennifer refused to give in. "Besides, a bandaged knee in nylons isn't exactly the fashion statement that I'm going for."

Sally reluctantly conceded the point. "Fine. But you'll be the only woman there who isn't wearing a dress," was Sally's parting shot.

Jennifer settled back into her pillow and closed her eyes. Without provocation, Heather's image came to mind. A warm glow settled over her as she allowed herself the simple luxury of thinking about Heather, remembering moments from the past and merging them with the images of today.

There was so much she wanted to ask her. So many thoughts and questions about her life and about their childhood. As dreams overtook her, she hoped fervently that she would get the chance.

Chapter 12

Jennifer arrived in the ballroom of the Hotel Savory well after the reception had begun. She chatted with a few people before finding an out of the way spot to settle down. She chose one of three couches that faced a roaring fireplace. From there she had a great view of the entrance, the bar, and the lounge area.

She sipped her drink and observed the decor of the hotel as much as the people who filled the room.

Was it just a coincidence that Sheila had rented a room at the same hotel where the evening's festivities were taking place? Jennifer didn't think so. In fact, she believed now more than ever that Sheila had taken some carefully orchestrated steps this weekend. She had definite plans for how she wanted the reunion to play out.

As she watched a group of people she couldn't quite identify, she tried to decipher her feelings for Sheila. Some emotions were easier to distinguish than others. At least she wasn't nervous anymore. The jitters she'd suffered ever since making her plane reservations had vanished. Even the confusion from earlier that morning had disappeared. She was thinking clearly now. Emotions from the past were no longer getting confused with the present.

Reality was what she'd needed. The confrontation with Sheila had left her feeling empty. Her anguish had vanished. She had no strong desire to be at Sheila's side. She had no yearning to whisk Sheila away.

Jennifer struggled with the realization. She'd been living with the hope and fantasy of Sheila all these years, and she didn't quite know what to do with the freedom that settled into her heart as the weight of Sheila's memory was lifted from her.

As if on cue, Sheila entered the ballroom, her arm through Bobby's. They joined a large group at the bar. Jen held her breath, waiting for her heart to pound. Relief washed over her, then elation. The emotion she felt had nothing to do with longing. In fact, as she watched Sheila laughing and flirting with the men that circled her and her husband, Jen felt something close to distaste.

She tried to name the emotion that surfaced. Regret? At the moment she regretted only two things.

The first regret was that she had let memories interfere with her life for so many years. The second regret was that she had met Sheila in her hotel room that morning.

It had probably helped her let go, however, Jen reasoned. If Sheila had remained cool and aloof, as she had been the night before, maybe Jen would be yearning for her even now.

"Alone at last." Diane's deep voice whispered in her ear, causing her to abandon her thoughts. Diane circled the sofa from behind and came around to sit beside her. Jennifer noted with satisfaction that Diane was wearing a pair of black tailored pants and a white blouse. She couldn't wait to tell Sally.

"How are you feeling?" Diane leaned forward to get a good look at the swollen lump above Jen's eye. "I didn't expect to see you tonight."

"I'm fine. And I wouldn't have missed this night for anything," she smiled.

Diane raised an eyebrow in reply. "Dare I ask?"

Jen waved the question aside. "Are you enjoying yourself so far?"

"It's been interesting to see everyone." Diane shrugged as she scanned the crowd. "I didn't have anything else to do this weekend."

"So you still live in Des Moines?"

Diane nodded. "I'm surprised how many of us still do, actually. Lucy's still here. Gina teaches up in Ames. Gail lives in Oskaloosa."

"Oskaloosa?"

"She married a farmer or something." Her face cracked in a wide smile. "My lover and I moved just south of Ankeny."

"Really?" It hadn't even occurred to her that

Diane might have a lover. "How long have you been together?"

Diane's smile grew even wider. "Eight years," she said proudly.

"Congratulations," Jen said with feeling. "Why didn't you bring her with you? I would have loved to meet her."

Diane's face colored. "Well, uh, she's here. You know her," she stuttered.

Jennifer stared at the larger woman, for the first time seeing her as someone's lover instead of as the high school lesbian. "Who? Who is it?"

"Well," she swallowed, dipping her head shyly. "It's Lucy."

Jennifer couldn't stop her jaw from dropping.

"But she's kind of closeted, ya know? So we play it cool."

Jennifer continued to stare. "Lucy?"

Diane's head bobbed up and down.

"That's fabulous." Jennifer finally found her voice. "She's an absolutely wonderful woman. Congratulations again."

"Thanks." She sat up proudly.

Amazed, Jen shook her head. "How did you two get together?"

Diane grinned broadly. "It's a long story. But that's part of what I wanted to talk to you about."

Jen remembered their brief conversation earlier in the day. "Ah yes. Your ominous warning."

"I thought you should know about a few things that happened since you moved away."

Her curiosity piqued, Jen asked her to continue.

"That first year you were away, after Sheila married that idiot and before they moved to Texas . . ."

Diane glanced around quickly before turning back to Jen, her voice low as she continued. "Sheila went pretty whacko when she couldn't find you. She called everybody and anybody to try to reach you. She was a maniac. She told everyone about the two of you. Well, her version of the story, anyway."

Jennifer digested the information slowly. "What was her version?"

"That you seduced her and fucked with her head before dumping her and running away."

"She got married." Jen's voice was louder than she'd intended.

Diane waved the comment aside. "I know. And nobody really believed her version of what happened anyway. Especially when they knew how much you were always mooning over her back in school."

Again the reminder that Jen had fooled absolutely no one in high school.

Diane hesitated for a moment. "Anyway, she finally told me a different story. One that's probably a whole lot closer to the truth."

Jen's eyes narrowed. "What did she tell you?"

Diane lowered her voice. "That you two had been lovers for years. That she couldn't handle being queer. So she married Bobby."

A low whistle escaped her. So many times she had imagined the reason, but she'd never heard the words before now. Jen looked away briefly, considering her words. But something didn't quite make sense.

"Why would she have told you? She wouldn't even give you the time of day in high school."

Diane's cheeks colored, and her eyes darted around nervously. "We became lovers," she confessed.

"After she was married. Once she realized that she wasn't going to get you back."

Jen heard a roaring in her ears at the same time and felt a sickening lurch in the pit of her stomach. She turned stinging eyes toward the flames in the fireplace beside them.

Diane continued. "We weren't lovers, exactly. We had an affair. All she talked about was you. Jenny this. Jenny that. I know she told that shithead husband of hers all about you. He went berserk. That's when they moved to Texas." She paused, her eyes turning to search for Sheila's whereabouts. "I'm surprised as hell that they came back here for the reunion. I would have thought his ego couldn't take it."

"Why are you telling me this?" The words came out more harshly than she'd intended.

Diane sighed. "Not to gloat, I assure you. I just feel like something's up, and I wanted to warn you. I figured that nobody else would tell you what happened back then. That she told everybody about you."

"That I seduced her," Jen said sarcastically. In her mind's eye, she imagined Sheila telling the story. She had no doubt that Sheila had spun it just as Diane was now telling her.

Diane nodded. "And I thought I should warn you, if you don't know already. Sheila's rented a room here. She has every intention of getting you up there alone."

Jennifer's stomach fluttered. "How do you know all of this?"

Diane's smile was steely. "Because she invited me there last night. And when I turned her down she made it quite clear that she'd rented it with you in mind anyway."

Jen watched her carefully, unable to speak.

"So, just a warning. She has plans for you." She smiled sweetly.

Duped. Completely, utterly fooled. Part of her wanted to confess to Diane that it was too late, but humiliation held her back.

When Jennifer didn't reply, Diane prompted her. "You're not still interested in her, are you?"

Jen shook her head slowly. "No. Not anymore." She turned her head toward the area where a small string quartet was beginning to play. Sheila was standing nearby, her eyes watching the two women covertly. "It's funny, though. I can see Sheila right now and believe that everything you're telling me is true. But I don't remember her being so manipulative back then. She was so sweet." Her eyes met Diane's. "She was my whole life."

Diane's lips were a careful straight line. "It hurts like hell, doesn't it," she said matter-of-factly.

An ironic smile twisted her lips. "It sure does."

"What hurts like hell?" Lucy was approaching them, looking a bit uncomfortable in a short beige cotton dress and heels.

"Love, sweetie." Diane smiled adoringly at her lover. "What else?"

"Lucy!" Jennifer pushed herself up from the couch and wrapped her arms around the shorter woman. "I'm so happy for you. Congratulations," she whispered.

Lucy practically beamed. "Thanks. I'm a lucky gal."

"I'd say you're both lucky," Jen smiled. "Sit down.

I want to hear all about you two." She motioned for Lucy to join Diane while she moved to another sofa beside them.

Slowly at first, the couple began telling their story, each interrupting the other as they wound the tale. Jennifer listened as they grew more animated, seeing the love clearly pouring from their eyes as they gazed at each other as their story continued.

Always a magnet, Lucy began to wave and draw others over to join them, and soon they were surrounded by friends from years ago. As topics became more general, Jennifer found herself growing restless, her eyes beginning to wander the growing crowd in search of Heather. And subconsciously for Sheila.

Trying to appear nonchalant, Jen's eyes began to scour the sea of faces in the crowded room. Surely Heather would have arrived by now.

Sheila, in contrast, was easy to spot. She continued to hold court at the bar, surrounded by men of all shapes and sizes, with her husband nearby. She seemed to be drinking heavily, and Jennifer absorbed this information with trepidation. A sober Sheila was tough enough to handle. She didn't even want to think about how difficult a drunk Sheila might be.

She allowed herself to be drawn back into the conversation at hand before beginning her search once again. She wasn't sure if she spotted the white-blond hair or the bright-blue eyes first. She was only aware of the breath that caught in her throat as she found Heather's eyes on hers from the farthest corner of the room.

My god, she's gorgeous. Jen was struck once again by the other woman's beauty. She was completely caught off guard and surprised at the way her heart thumped in her chest as Heather tilted her head and smiled in acknowledgment. Jen found herself smiling in return and she lifted her glass in salute. They continued to stare, eyes unwavering, and familiar strings tugged at Jennifer's heart. She tried without success to stifle the grin that spread across her face.

She wasn't sure whether she imagined that Heather was flirting with her, even at this distance. Her eyes seemed to smolder — not with lust or passion, but with something softer. A yearning of sorts. A heart-on-one's-sleeve kind of look.

She wasn't imagining it, Jen told herself. Heather felt the attraction too. Without another thought, Jen waved Heather over.

She tried to appear interested in the conversation around her, but her senses were centered on the blond head that was weaving its way through the throngs of people.

As Heather approached, Jennifer found herself unable to focus on anything else. Heather moved gracefully, the folds of her long white dress caressing tanned calves with each step. The sleeveless dress exposed smooth, slender arms and shoulders, its low cut exposing the hollow of her throat. White-blond hair was pulled back in a single French braid, displaying high cheekbones. Aqua-blue eyes, wide, expressive, shy and then playful, met Jen's with each step.

At last she was beside the sofa, gazing at Jennifer with a hesitant, teasing smile.

Jennifer realized she'd been holding her breath, and she exhaled slowly, recognizing the light-headedness that came over her.

"You look absolutely stunning." The words

tumbled from her lips unchecked. Heather accepted the compliment easily before letting her eyes travel the length of the other woman's body.

"You look awfully nice yourself," she replied, and Jennifer was at once thankful that she'd allowed her sister to convince her to borrow the linen pantsuit she was wearing.

A round of greetings echoed as Lucy urged Heather to join them.

"I'm not intruding?"

"Of course not." Jennifer found her voice and averted her eyes long enough to make room on the couch beside her. Jennifer became instantly focused on the knee that pressed lightly against her own.

"How long have you been here?" Aware of the many pairs of eyes around them, Jennifer tried to keep her voice light.

"Oh," Heather cringed. "About an hour."

"An hour? Why didn't you come over sooner?"

Long lashes fluttered down. "Sometimes the old me rears its ugly head." She forced a laugh. "I was feeling a little shy," she admitted.

Jennifer saw a brief glimpse of the timid Heather of years ago. Then she was reminded of the short time left in the weekend, and she rushed to reassure her. "Don't be shy." She dropped her voice. "I've been waiting for you all evening. I couldn't wait to see you again." She stopped herself abruptly, realizing that she was saying more than she'd intended.

Heather leaned closer, the palm of her hand pressing lightly on Jen's knee. "You mean my confession didn't scare you off?" she whispered, her lips just barely brushing Jennifer's ear.

Jen laughed as a tingle shot up her spine.

"Absolutely not. In fact" — she swallowed hard, shyness upon her — "I was kind of hoping . . ." Her smile faltered as she found herself staring into the bluest, most earnest eyes she'd ever seen.

Everything and everyone around them seemed to fade, until she was aware only of the face inches from her own, of the overwhelming desire to wrap her arms around this woman and hold her. Just hold her. In the softest and gentlest way imaginable.

Jennifer felt her cheeks grow hot, and she dropped her eyes.

"Now who's shy?" Heather raised an eyebrow, teasing her.

Too aware of the others around them, a proper retort eluded Jennifer. They continued to steal glances at each other, smiling secretly, as Lucy's voice drifted over them.

"Looks like they're serving dinner. Are you two coming?"

Heather was the first to break their gaze. "Of course," she said smoothly. "Will you save us two places? I just want to catch up on something with Jenny first."

Jennifer smiled sheepishly as she realized that the room must have been emptying for some time. While she'd been so focused on Heather, almost everyone had been moving toward the dining room. She hadn't even noticed.

Chapter 13

They took their time making their way to dinner, both reluctant to break the spell. Heather suggested a short stroll and led them beyond the string quartet, who were beginning to pack up their instruments, and past the lounge area. She reached for the door-knobs of two French doors, pausing long enough to wiggle her eyebrows at Jennifer before pushing the doors wide open.

Cool night air sent goose bumps along Jen's skin as they stepped out on the balcony.

"The Des Moines skyline," Heather swept her arms wide.

Jennifer moved to the balcony's edge, placing the palms of her hands on the railing as she looked out over the night.

"It's changed, hasn't it?" she murmured, struck by the number of bright lights and the traffic on the streets below.

Heather nodded in agreement, joining her at the railing. "They've really built it up. It's not the way I remember it at all."

"It's pretty, but it makes me sad." She looked down at the streets, trying to identify different landmarks. "It's scary that some things have changed so much."

"Even scarier how some things have stayed the same." Heather's voice held an ironic twist.

Jennifer considered the shorter woman, becoming aware of her closeness, of the perfume that floated over her. Heather's eyes were trained on the streets below, a pensive look covering her features. For the umpteenth time that day, the urge to hold Heather nearly overwhelmed Jennifer.

Again she felt the pressure of time upon her, and she found a courage that normally would have eluded her. She turned to face Heather, hesitating only a moment before reaching out to cover Heather's hand with her own. She was rewarded with fingers curling around hers, and the sight of Heather's downturned head looking at their entwined fingers with amazement.

Heather's tongue slipped across her lips. "Am I imagining this?"

Jennifer's smile came slowly, bubbling in her chest

before finally spilling out on her lips as she shook her head. "You mean it's not just me?"

Something near relief swept Heather's features. "No. It's definitely not just you."

They stood without moving, awkwardly meeting each other's gaze. "This is scary." Heather shivered, retrieving her hand and reaching up to hug her upper arms.

A number of thoughts crowded Jen's mind, and her soaring hopes began to ebb. "But why?" he prompted, touching a single finger to Heather's forearm.

Heather's eyes dropped to where skin met skin before raising her eyes to meet Jennifer's.

"This wasn't supposed to happen. You were supposed to be living happily in New York with your lover, and I was supposed to feel absolutely no attraction to you whatsoever. I wanted to be able to look you in the eye and say to myself, See, it was nothing. That crush you had all those years ago was nothing more than that."

Jen felt a grin involuntarily tug at the corners of her mouth, and her heart began to sing.

"And?"

"And nothing," Heather said. "I've already said too much."

Jen responded by chuckling softly. "So you thought you'd take one look and wonder what you ever saw in me."

"Something like that," Heather admitted grudgingly, without bothering to hide her smile. "Are you sure you don't have some woman tucked away somewhere back home?"

"No one," Jennifer laughed, thoroughly enjoying

herself. "I haven't even been on a date in two years. What about you?"

Heather shook her head. "It's just me and Amy."

Their fingers met again, resuming their dance.

"I really do want to see you again. When we get back home," Jen told her.

"I'd like that very much." She tipped her head to one side. "When is your flight tomorrow?"

"Two o'clock. What about you? Are you flying into Phoenix?"

Heather nodded. "Yes. But we're leaving in the morning. Around eight o'clock, I think."

Disappointed, Jen was surprised by her own sudden anxiety, wanting to arrange something more concrete. "You'll probably be in Flagstaff by the time my plane lands . . ." She let the sentence dangle, hoping that Heather wouldn't let the weekend end.

"Probably," she agreed. "What about next weekend? Are you free?"

"Absolutely. Will you and Amy come down?"

"She would love that. *I* would love that."

Jen smiled as she rocked back on her heels. They watched each other shyly, eyes dropping to where their fingers continued touching.

Jen felt herself sobering, Heather's closeness drawing her in. "Should we go back and join the others now?" she asked.

Heather wrinkled her nose, considering the question. "I'm not in any hurry," she answered, her voice dropping down conspiratorially. "I feel like we're playing hooky or something. I rather like it."

Jennifer laughed. "You never skipped school, did you?"

Heather grimaced. "No. I was so straightlaced. But *you* did, didn't you."

"Guilty," Jen admitted.

Heather tipped her head provocatively, looking squarely into Jennifer's eyes as she moved even closer. "And is this what it felt like?"

She felt Heather's breath on her cheek. "And how does this feel, exactly?"

Heather considered the question for a brief moment before replying. "Heady. Kind of naughty." She grinned as she finished.

Jennifer raised one fine brow. "Naughty? This feels naughty?" She allowed herself to be drawn in, eyes trained now on the mouth that hovered just inches from her own.

"Kind of." The reply was a near whisper. Dark lashes fluttered down as she leaned in to receive Jen's lips with her own.

The kiss was soft, hesitant and lingering; the lips barely touched. Jen's knees grew weak as a mixture of delight and euphoria settled over her.

She stood transfixed even as Heather's lips left hers and she found herself staring down into those large eyes. Her own reaction caught her off guard, causing her to stare with wonder.

Her mood threatened to grow serious, and she failed miserably at an attempted smile.

A small crease found its way between Heather's brows. "That's a pretty serious look."

"Hmm." Jen let out the breath that she'd been holding. "You were right. This is scary."

"But okay?"

"Very okay." She fought the urge to reach out and stroke the blond hair that framed Heather's head.

"Do you still regret coming back?" Heather was smiling provocatively.

"Did I say that?"

"You did."

"Couldn't have been me. Are you sure there's no one else here that you had a crush on?"

Heather was quick to put a finger to Jen's ribs before sliding her arms around her waist and finding her lips once again. This time not so gently.

Chapter 14

Dinner turned out to be far more pleasant than Jen had hoped. Having Heather at her side added an unexpected nuance to the evening. There was no lack of subtle touches. A light hand on her arm, a knee pressed against hers, gentle reminders that the weekend had taken a strange and wondrous twist.

Diane and Lucy had picked up on it instantly, sliding knowing glances in Jennifer's direction as they joined the others at the table. Food, laughter, and wine floated among them. Memories were stirred and moments relived. All the while Jennifer was aware of Heather beside her. Of the blue eyes that found hers each time she glanced around. She felt torn between wanting the evening to end, and wanting it to go on forever.

When the banquet tables were cleared, the class president rose to act as emcee for a number of the old classmates who spoke to the attendees. Afterward, the group was dismissed to the ballroom, where dancing and drinking began in earnest.

Jennifer was ready to leave at the end of the official festivities, but the small group convinced Heather and her to stay a while longer. They made their way back to the lounge area, spying the couches that surrounded the fireplace and electing Jen to fetch a round of drinks before joining them.

Heather volunteered to help her, and they made their way through the crowded room to stand in line at the bar.

"I must admit that I've had a wonderful time this evening." Heather placed a casual hand on Jennifer's arm, leaning over so that she whispered the words in Jen's ear. "But I think I'd like to go soon. Maybe we could go somewhere quiet for a while."

Jennifer tilted her head and smiled. "That would be nice. Why don't we join them for one drink and then leave?"

They were jostled from all sides as bodies pressed against them, pushing them together. They became aware of the others that surrounded them, mostly men, becoming raucous and boisterous.

"Excuse me." A male voice intruded just as Jen saw the masculine hand on Heather's arm.

Jennifer didn't need the name tag to identify Dan

Johnson. He was slightly taller and more muscular than she remembered. A full mustache covered his upper lip but didn't hide the dimples that still punctuated his cheeks.

Each woman stared at him expectantly, but his eyes never left Heather's face as he pointedly ignored Jennifer.

"I'm hoping you can settle an argument that my buddy and I are having." He gestured over his shoulder to another man that stood several feet away.

Jennifer threw the other man a cursory glance before returning her attention fully to Dan Johnson. Old anger and new jealousy began mixing in her gut. She observed what she interpreted as pure lust on Dan's features as he continued to flash his smile at Heather. She imagined what Heather might be thinking.

Heather was returning his gaze, her eyes alert but carefully hooded.

"Neither one of us can seem to place you, and so I've come to the conclusion that you couldn't possibly have gone to Washington when we did." He was leaning forward, ignoring the way Jen had moved a little closer to Heather.

"Really. Why?" Heather found her voice, her words tentative.

Dan's smile became a little wider. "Because there is no way that I could have gone to that school for four years without noticing someone as gorgeous as you." He continued to smile, one eyelid dropping down in a flirtatious wink.

Jennifer wanted to wipe the smirk from his face. But Heather was returning his smile, causing panic to rise along Jen's spine.

"That's quite interesting." Heather's voice was honey sweet. "Because I was definitely there."

Jennifer blinked hard, not believing her eyes. Heather was actually flirting with him. Confusion gripped her mind as she continued to watch the pair trade coy smiles and ogling stares.

"Really?" Dan managed to lean in just a bit closer.

"Uh-huh," Heather nodded. "And I definitely remember you." Her words lilted wickedly, causing a knife to twist in Jennifer's chest.

Dan drew himself up, preening as his chin jutted out. His smile grew salacious.

As the pair continued to size each other up, Jennifer stared, seething at the way Heather had cast her aside so abruptly. Jennifer had kissed Heather only an hour ago! Jennifer stared at the seductive smile meant not for her, but for this man, and felt the heat rising along the back of her neck. Then her eyes lifted, tracing the curve of Heather's cheek, coming to rest on her eyes.

Her eyes. Not smoldering. Not teasing. Not playful. Cold eyes. Steely eyes. A grin sprang to Jennifer's lips as she recognized her own mistake. Quite an actress, Jen thought, as she braced herself, eager to see just how Heather would play out the charade.

"So where's your name tag?" Dan asked coyly, his cheeks dimpling. "Did we know each other in school?"

"Oh yes," Heather nodded. "We knew each other."

Dan's expression showed frustration as he shook his head. "Did we go out?"

Jennifer nearly choked.

"No." Heather chuckled, content to draw him out. Then she lifted a hand to draw Jennifer closer, drawing her into their conversation as she continued to smile graciously. "Do you remember Jenny Moreland?"

Dan's smile faltered as his eyes floated over Jen. "Sure." He nodded a hesitant greeting, which Jennifer returned. She noted with satisfaction that he seemed to grow edgy.

"Who are you?" His eyes narrowed as his attention swept back to Heather.

"I'm Heather O'Brien." She smiled sweetly while Jennifer's eyes glittered with anticipation. *This is too good.*

Dan squinted, shaking his head. "I'm sorry," he began. "But I can't place you. Are you sure that I knew you?"

"Positive." This time Jennifer's voice chimed in with Heather's.

"You know, Danny," Heather's voice dropped down. "I must admit that I'm a little disappointed that you don't remember me."

Dan dipped his head in an appropriate aw-shucks response.

"Especially when you had such a tremendous impact on my teenage years," Heather continued.

Now Dan was preening again.

"Now I remember." Heather reached up and tapped her palm to her forehead as if a realization had suddenly occurred to her. "You probably only remember me by my nickname."

"Your nickname."

"Yep. I'll bet that's it." Her smile never faltered as she continued. "You used to call me Tracks, Danny. Isn't that right, Jenny?"

Jennifer knew immense satisfaction as she watched his face fall.

"Yep," Jen drew the syllable out slowly. "That's what he called you."

Dan's face grew white. "No. You can't be her. She was —"

"Homely?" Heather finished the sentence for him, the sweet smile never leaving her face. "I believe you called me that as well. You know, Danny," she lowered her voice until it was nearly seductive. "I can't tell you how many nights I cried myself to sleep over the cruel things you used to say and do to me. But as you can see, I turned out just fine." Without missing a beat, she raised her voice again to a normal tone. "Do you have any children, Danny?"

"No." Confused, he stared back at her with horror as he shook his head.

Heather managed her brightest smile yet. "That's probably a blessing, you know. After all, if there's anyone here who shouldn't procreate, it's you." She blinked her eyes sweetly. "It's been a pleasure catching up with you, Danny. And now if you'll excuse us." Her nod was abrupt as she turned away swiftly and stepped forward toward the bar.

Stunned, Jennifer followed her lead and stared straight ahead as she replayed the conversation in her mind. A moment passed before she let out a soft whistle.

"Remind me never to piss you off," she said under her breath, for Heather's ears only. She expected to hear Heather's laughter, but quickly turned to look at the other woman when she received no reply.

Heather had gone white, and Jen could see that her hands were shaking.

"Are you okay?" Concern enveloped her, and she reached out a hand to steady her.

Heather ran her tongue over her bottom lip. "Yeah. I'm just a little shaky." The blue eyes that lifted to Jen's were wide with something close to remorse. "I was mean, wasn't I?" She was shaking her head. "I shouldn't have said those things."

"You were perfect." Jen rushed to reassure her. "He deserved it."

"He's probably a really nice guy. All that old shit was years ago." Her voice was heavy with uncertainty.

"Hey." Jen turned so that she faced her fully, not caring what the others around them might be thinking. "You're right. He might very well be a nice guy now. But he wasn't then. And if he is such a great guy today, then he'll recognize why you said what you did." She searched Heather's eyes, feeling inadequate. "I'm proud of you. Closure. Remember?"

Heather blinked several times before a small laugh fell from her lips. "Did you see the way his face dropped?"

"I sure did." Jen gave her a quick hug. "I can't wait to get to know you better," she smiled. "I think I'm going to enjoy it immensely."

Heather raised an eyebrow, her lips curving in a knowing smile. "I'm enjoying it already."

Jennifer felt a sharp pang of arousal as she stared into Heather's eyes. The effect was delicious. "I can't wait to get out of here," she whispered.

"Me, either." She glanced across the room to where Lucy and Diane were holding court. "I'm still a little shaky, though. Do you mind if I go sit down for a bit?"

"Go ahead. I'll get their drinks and be right over."

"Are you sure?"

"Positive," Jen assured her. She watched as Heather walked away, feeling her absence immediately.

The line was moving too slowly, and Jennifer grew impatient. Her mind wandered to Dan Johnson, then somehow to Sheila.

Unreasonable panic seized her. She didn't want to be alone. She didn't want to have any opportunity to run into Sheila. A sense of foreboding came over her as she looked around. Just as she'd guessed, Sheila wasn't far away.

Yikes. Jen wasn't sure if Sheila had spotted her or not, but she wasn't willing to take any chances. She knew Sheila would find her. The last thing she wanted was a moment alone with Sheila. With or without an audience. Jen was sure that it would only lead to another confrontation, and she wasn't ready to test her newfound freedom face-to-face.

It seemed like a good time to make a detour to the ladies room, and she tried making herself as inconspicuous as possible as she threaded her way through the bar crowd.

The door loomed before her, and she grabbed for it, breathing a sigh of relief as she stepped inside the lounge area apparently unnoticed. She stood there for a moment, collecting her thoughts and glancing around. The lounge area was small, with one couch and a large makeup area before a wall-size mirror. A separate doorway led to the lavatory.

Jen took a deep breath and realized that her hands were shaking. She was angry with herself for running. *Running.* Anxiety crushed the air from her lungs as she berated herself.

The door to the hallway opened slowly. Jennifer held her breath as Sheila made her entrance.

Damn. Damn. Damn.

"You've been avoiding me," Sheila purred, her smile lazy as the door closed behind her and she stepped to within arm's length of Jennifer.

Funny, Jen thought. *Up until about five minutes ago, I hadn't given Sheila a second thought in hours.* "No. I haven't," she said honestly.

Sheila brushed the comment aside. "No matter. I've got you now." She stepped forward, far too close as far as Jen was concerned. "Here, I brought you something." She held out a fisted hand and waited for Jen to raise hers.

Reluctantly, Jen lifted her hand. Two seconds later, a large brass key rested in her palm.

"What time can you meet me?" Sheila asked sweetly.

"I can't." Jen said the words as firmly as she could muster while trying to return the key to Sheila's hand.

"Don't tease me, Jenny. I won't beg." Sheila's voice sounded slurred as she reached up to trace Jen's chin with one finger. "Unless, of course, it makes you hot. Is that what you want, Jenny baby?" She was so close now that Jen could smell the alcohol on her breath.

Jennifer kept her arms carefully at her sides, refusing to react as she felt the tension building along her spine.

Sheila's fingers dropped down, tracing the collar of Jen's blouse before brushing across one breast.

"Let's play doctor, Jenny. Or do you have a better game in mind?" Her breath was hot on Jen's cheek. Jennifer clenched her jaw as she struggled with the conflicting emotions that kept her immobilized. Repulsion, anger, and frustration clashed with quick, hot arousal as Sheila's hand dropped to Jen's crotch.

"Stop it, Sheila," she croaked. She could tell by her smile that Sheila thought she'd won. And Jen wasn't so sure that she hadn't. Sheila pressed the length of her body against Jen's, her large breasts pushing against Jen's chest as her hand continued to play between Jen's legs.

"Let me fuck you, baby. Please." Her voice was gruff, somewhere between a demand and a plea.

Jennifer's head spun as her senses collided. The voice in her head screamed for Sheila to stop — while the ache between her legs begged Sheila to fuck her fast and hard.

She lifted her leaden arms, palms finding her shoulders.

"Sheila. I said no." Jen shook her head, forcing arousal aside as she pushed Sheila just beyond reach.

Sheila's brown eyes were wide and wounded, staring back at Jen as if she'd just been hit.

"You've never said no to me," she said quietly, curiously. She seemed dazed, and Jen seized the moment to catch her breath and steady herself.

"What did you say to Bobby, Sheila? Why did he come after me today?"

Sheila wasn't hearing Jen's words. She seemed to be talking to herself, her lips moving soundlessly. The puzzled look remained on her features.

"You've never said no to me," she repeated aloud. Jen grew uneasy. As if a light went off somewhere in her mind, Sheila's head snapped back and her eyes glared into Jen's.

"It's that woman. Tracks." She threw back her head and laughed.

Anger exploded behind Jen's eyes.

"It is, isn't it? That slut," she spat.

Jennifer felt her hands clenching as she fought to control the seething in her belly.

"You're pushing me too far, Sheila." Jennifer said the words slowly, succinctly. "Heather has nothing to do with this."

Again Sheila seemed not to hear as her bitter laughter echoed in the small room. "That's good. That's rich, Jenny." She stepped forward again, her voice dropping to a menacing octave. "Did you tell her that you fucked me this morning? Did you tell her how good it felt to have me in your arms again?"

Jen hated her. She wanted to slap her. She wanted to reach inside of her own body and rip Sheila's memory from her heart and throw it to the ground.

A toilet flushed.

Oh christ. Someone was hearing their conversation, had heard every word.

An evil smirk settled on Sheila's face, and triumphant laughter gurgled in her throat.

"Caught red-handed, lover." She dangled the last word sarcastically before raising her voice. "I'll be waiting for you, darlin'. You've got the key," she called, before spinning away to pull open the door and step out into the hallway.

The sudden quiet was deafening as panic seized Jen. Should she make a quick exit herself? Or should she stay and find out who had witnessed the little scene.

She glanced down, and her fist uncurled to expose the brass key that had impressed the palm of her hand. She dropped the key to the carpeted floor and watched it bounce once before she reached for the door.

She was chicken. And she'd had enough of this class reunion shit.

Chapter 15

"Where's Heather?" Jennifer made a beeline straight to Diane Miller. She was milling about with some others beside the fireside lounge.

"I thought she was with you," she smiled. "We were all thinking about taking off. Wanna join us?"

Jennifer was already scoping the crowd, searching for Heather's familiar features. "Maybe. I need to find Heather." Jen turned to walk away, but Diane's hand on her arm stopped her cold.

"Whoa." She squinted her eyes, raking them over Jen's features. "You look like you've seen a ghost."

"Yeah. A ghost named Sheila." Her eyes searched nervously. *Where is Heather?* "I want to get out of here."

"Had enough?" Lucy approached, smiling as always.

"I'm afraid so," Jen grimaced. "I want to find Heather before I leave."

"Here she is." Diane was looking over Jen's shoulder, and Jen turned to see Heather coming their way, a glass of wine in one hand. Relief washed over her.

"Are you ready to go?" Jen called when Heather was barely within shouting distance. Her voice was anxious.

She was nodding, and Jen grew impatient as she took her time saying good-bye to everyone. Finally they were leaving, making their way through the ballroom, and down the long corridor toward the hotel lobby.

Heather seemed strangely quiet, and Jen's thoughts raced with paranoia. "Where are you parked?"

"Across the street. In the garage."

Was she imagining the coolness in Heather's voice?

"Would you like to go somewhere for coffee?" While Jen was eager for the reunion to be over, she wasn't ready to say good night to Heather. Too many things were happening. She wanted suddenly to tell Heather about Sheila. Everything. About the scene just now in the rest room, about that morning, about everything that had happened years ago.

"I think I should probably be getting back. It's getting late, and my flight leaves early tomorrow."

They had reached the lobby, and Heather stopped so that they faced each other. Heather's features were closed, her lips unsmiling.

Desperation welled up inside of Jen.

"I know it sounds silly" — she forced a laugh she didn't feel — "but I don't think I'm ready to let you go."

One fine brow raised ever so slightly as one side of Heather's mouth lifted. "And I don't think you're ready to let anybody go." Her words, although spoken without a hint of sarcasm, sent tremors through Jennifer's body.

Dumbstruck, Jen stared at her stupidly, waiting for her to continue.

"Haven't dated anyone in two years, huh?" Sarcasm was finally sneaking into her voice. "I guess you weren't counting one-night stands. Or should I say one-morning stands?"

Jen's mind tumbled. Caught so completely off-guard, she struggled to understand. She continued to stare at Heather, watching as she reached out and dropped something into Jen's hand.

The brass key to Sheila's room.

"I think you dropped this in the rest room." Now her voice was quiet and controlled.

Jen's heart dropped to her stomach. A groan started deep in her throat. "Heather. Let me explain." Jennifer reached for her arm, and Heather stiffened.

"You don't have to, Jenny." She sounded tired. "Like I said before — some things never change."

"But they do." Jen knew she was whining when she felt the stares of the desk clerk and the bellhop on her neck. She dropped her voice. "Please. Let's go somewhere to talk."

Heather shook her head, looking suddenly exhausted.

"Jenny!" Diane Miller's insistent voice was behind them. "Jenny!"

Jen pulled her eyes from Heather's just as Diane reached them. She was huffing and puffing, clearly out of breath.

"I'm sorry. But you've got to come back in —"

"We're leaving."

"No." Diane's hand clamped down on Jen's wrist. "I'm sorry. But you have to. Sheila's flipping out. She's ranting and raving at the top of her lungs."

Jen knew her face went white. "Why me?"

Diane was tugging on my wrist now. "Because it's your name she's yelling."

Heather's lips were a tight, straight line.

"Come on, Jenny," Diane was saying. "You know I wouldn't drag you back in to that woman for anything less than an emergency."

Jen knew she was right. Heather was raising both hands, palms out. "Just like old times."

The words stung Jennifer. "Please don't go," she implored. "I'll be right back." Jen's feet were already tripping over themselves as Diane dragged her away.

Expecting that a thundering noise would greet them when they reached the ballroom, Jen was surprised by the silence that hung over the faces that turned their way. A large group had congregated behind the bar, their necks craning to get a better view of what was happening on the balcony beyond the French doors.

Jen followed Diane as she pushed each one aside until they were standing on the threshold of the balcony. It took several moments for Jen's eyes to grow accustomed to the darkness. Her lungs sucked in the cold air as she took in the scene before them.

Lucy was there, tugging unsuccessfully on the arm of a man, trying to pull him back to the door.

"She's my wife," Bobby was saying. He shrugged Lucy off and moved forward, reaching down as he went.

Jen's eyes followed Bobby's outstretched arm, her stomach lurching as she spotted Sheila. She was huddled in the corner of the balcony, hair strewn wildly and makeup smeared across her face. Her already short skirt fell back around her thighs as she kicked outward, striking Bobby's hand.

"Don't touch me," she hissed, her fists flailing as Bobby bent over her. "Stay away from me!" She was screeching and howling obscenities repeatedly, causing each of the others to cringe in response.

Jen glanced to Gina, Lucy, and then Diane before turning back to Sheila and Bobby.

"Bobby." Diane called his name in a controlled voice before stepping out into the fray. She reached for his shoulder. "Bobby."

He turned to face her, his wounded face contorted in pain. As Diane spoke to him quietly, Jen's eyes fell back to Sheila, who continued to wail at the top of her lungs.

Bobby was eyeing Jennifer now, and for the first time in Jen's life, she actually felt sympathy for the man. She nodded quietly before taking a deep breath and gingerly stepping outside.

Sheila was sobbing quietly now, so that all Jen could hear was Bobby's deep breaths as she inched past him. Gauging herself to be at least an arm's length away, Jen crouched down to observe Sheila more closely.

"Sheila?" Jen said her name quietly. When no response came, she repeated the name again.

Swollen eyes fluttered open.

"Jenny?" Tears sprang again, sending even more makeup streaming down her cheeks. "You came back."

Jennifer smiled gently, her heart constricting. "Of course I did."

"But I saw you leaving with her." She was wiping her nose on the sleeve of her blouse, trying without success to straighten her hair.

"I'm right here, Sheila." She felt guilty, hating the sound of her own voice, hating the lie that she was implying.

"You didn't leave me." Fresh tears sprang in her eyes and she rubbed them furiously.

Jennifer could smell the alcohol, even from that distance. Sheila was stinking drunk.

Jen glanced back over her shoulder, nodding curtly at Diane and Bobby, whose eyes she couldn't meet. When she turned back to Sheila, she knew that Diane was convincing Bobby to back off.

"Come hold me, Jenny." Sheila patted the concrete slab beside her. "Please?"

Jen hesitated. "Sheila," she said quietly, her voice caressing the name. "I think you've had too much to drink."

Sheila giggled.

"How about some coffee? Would you like that?"

"Will you drink with me?" She sounded like a child.

"Of course. Right out here on the balcony." She threw a glance back over her shoulder and knew that Lucy was scampering to find some coffee.

"Hold me?" Sheila's arms were outstretched, her streaked face that of a scared, pathetic child as she begged the question again. "Please?"

The image of Sheila shook Jen. With a heavy heart, she nodded, then knelt to take Sheila in her arms.

They held each other tightly, rocking slowly, oblivious to onlookers. They huddled together, arms wrapped tightly as they sat in silence.

Lucy came with a large pot of coffee and left after pouring two cups. Gina appeared with a large blanket, which Jennifer accepted and tucked around the two of them. Wordlessly, she held Sheila while she watched Diane shooing everyone away from the doors. Finally, only two pairs of eyes were peeking through the curtains at the two women, and Jen knew they belonged to Bobby and Diane.

Well over an hour and a full pot of coffee had passed before Sheila lifted her head from Jen's shoulder and sighed loudly.

"I really made a mess tonight, Jenny." She sounded tired and resigned. Traces of her earlier drunkenness had evaporated.

Cautiously, Jen searched for a reply. "Let's just say you were the hit of the party," she said softly.

Sheila chuckled, appreciating Jen's humor, before growing somber once again. "My life just seems to be one fuckup after another."

Jennifer remained quiet, letting Sheila continue.

"I never meant to hurt you when we were kids, Jenny. I loved you more than anything." She was shaking her head. "I just didn't have the strength. Bobby asked me to marry him, and I thought it was what I was supposed to do. It was a mistake. One mistake on top of another."

Jennifer searched for optimistic words. "But I'm sure he loves you, Sheila."

"I know he does. Even after all the hell I've put him through. But you were right this morning." She shifted a bit, so that she could better face the other woman.

Jennifer tried, but couldn't recall what she had said earlier that day. Even that morning felt years and years ago.

"You were right when you said I shouldn't stay with him if I'm still attracted to women." She eyed Jen openly, regret plain on her face. "I've been searching for another Jenny Moreland since the day I got married. Pretty pathetic, huh?"

Jennifer was careful not to agree or disagree. The truth was that even now she felt torn. She wanted to tell her how much she'd hurt over the years. How much she had longed to be with her again. But another part of her took a sick pleasure in knowing that Sheila had also suffered. But more than anything, she just wanted to let go. "I don't know anything about your relationship with your husband." She chose her words carefully. "I only know that you don't seem very happy. You have to go with your heart, I guess."

"And if it leads me to you?" Sheila countered.

A breeze picked up, sending a shiver down

Jennifer's spine as she mulled over her reply. "It took me a very, very long time to get over you, Sheila." She met Sheila's eyes squarely, unable to control the unabashed hurt in her own. "But I have. I couldn't go back now."

Sheila digested this with a shrug and a smile. "It would never work anyway. We've both moved on."

Jennifer nodded, the quiet settling between them once more. "What are you going to do?"

"Nothing," Sheila sighed. "I've got a husband and three boys to worry about. And I just made an absolute fool of myself." She groaned. "I think I've got to pee, darlin'."

Jennifer laughed and slowly unwound her stiff joints to stand. She was conscious of the door opening and three figures stepping outside as she reached down to help Sheila to her feet.

"I'm sorry, Jenny." Sheila's arms wrapped around her tightly, and Jennifer allowed herself to squeeze the other woman in return. "For everything."

In another moment, Jennifer's arms were empty, with nothing but the Des Moines skyline before her. Tears were threatening, and she stabbed at her eyes angrily as Bobby wrapped his arms around his wife and walked off with her.

"Are you okay?" Diane and Lucy stood a short distance away.

Jennifer nodded, failing at her attempt to smile. "She was a mess, huh?"

Diane was nodding. "Thanks for coming back."

"Sure," she nodded with finality. "Let's get out of here."

The ballroom had emptied in her absence. Jennifer glanced around only briefly when she reached the lobby. She hadn't really expected Heather to be there waiting, anyway.

Chapter 16

She tried without success to sneak into her sister's house without making a sound. But Sally, draped in a cotton bathrobe, had followed her to her bedroom, before she even had a chance to kick off her shoes.

"What happened to my suit?" Sally's voice was groggy with sleep.

Eyes wide, Jen glanced down to see the front of the suit smeared with makeup. One sleeve was caked with heavy brown foundation, and one lapel was streaked with black mascara.

"Shit. It's Sheila's makeup." She hurried to shrug out of the jacket, grimacing as Sally grabbed it for inspection.

"Christ, Jenny. What the hell did you do?" She threw her sister a disgusted look before holding out one hand and turning her face away. "Never mind. I don't want to know."

Recognizing the direction that Sally's thoughts had taken, Jennifer was quick to come to her own defense. "It's not what you think. She was crying. She was a mess." She bent to look closer at the damaged suit. "I'm sorry about the suit. I'll pay to have it cleaned."

"And I'll let you," Sally retorted, dropping the jacket in a heap to the floor. She faced her sister, pulling the robe tightly around her and shading her eyes from the bright light. "What the hell happened? It's almost three o'clock."

Jennifer groaned. "It's late. I'll tell you about it tomorrow."

Sally responded by plopping herself down on Jen's bed and making herself comfortable. "Tomorrow the kids will be demanding attention, and you'll be getting on a plane back to Phoenix. I want to spend time with my sister." She pouted as she patted the bed beside her. "Humor me."

Jennifer smiled as she joined her sister on the bed. Jennifer recounted the events of the past several hours.

Some twenty minutes later, she dropped her head on her pillow, tired from the retelling.

"Is your life always this tumultuous?" Sally asked.

"I notice you didn't use the word *exciting*." Jen

was able to find her sense of humor. "But no. My life is usually quite dull."

"What are you going to do about Heather?"

"I don't know." Frowning, Jen shook her head. "I don't even have her phone number." Her heart was sinking. Even if she *did* find her, she didn't know if she could find the words to make things right.

Her waking thoughts were of Heather. Maybe she could change her flight. Maybe she could drive over to the airport and catch her before she boarded the plane.

That's it! Her eyes flew open, and she threw back the blankets in a single motion. One hand reached for a bathrobe while the other grabbed her watch from the nightstand.

"Nine-thirty." She blinked hard, not trusting her eyes. "Shit. She's already over Saint Louis by now. Shit. Shit. Shit." She fell back against her pillow. She stared up at the ceiling, her thoughts drifting back over the night before. She wondered about Sheila, how she was, how she was coping.

She waited to feel the familiar ache that always came with the memory of Sheila, but she felt nothing.

It was a somber group that hovered around the boarding gate at the Des Moines airport.

Jennifer always hated it when it was time to say

good-bye, and this time was no exception. In fact, it was worse. Her heart was heavy.

Sally was sniffling. Allison had taken up her favorite position behind her mother's leg. Tommy sat securely in his father's arms, pointing that single finger right at her and repeating her name over and over. "Jeffer. Jeffer. Jeffer." Giggles erupted.

The flight attendant was saying that all passengers holding a boarding pass should be enplaning. Not wanting to prolong the inevitable any longer, Jennifer began her good-byes.

She hugged Jim quickly. She felt the first threat of tears when Tommy planted a wet, sloppy kiss on her mouth and hugged her tightly.

Jennifer squatted down, taking one last shot at trying to coax her niece out from behind her mother's leg.

"By, Allison," she tried. "I'll see you at Christmas, okay?"

Wide brown eyes stared back at her for several moments. Feeling rejected once more, Jen stood up, completely caught off guard when Allison dashed around Sally to throw herself into Jennifer's arms.

"I don't want you to leave." She was crying, tears rolling down round cheeks. Small fists clutched at the short hair on Jennifer's head, refusing to let go.

"Allison, I'll be back. I promise." Jennifer felt her eyes stinging in earnest.

"No, you won't," she pouted. Full, tiny lips were pulled down in a frown. "You always stay away forever."

Jennifer eyed the little girl. It hadn't even occurred to her that Allison might remember her from her last visit. "Do you remember the last time I was here?"

Allison nodded, fresh tears bursting and spilling over her cheeks. "Mommy cried when you went away. You made her sad."

Jennifer lifted soulful eyes to her sister's, and saw Sally's tears. Sally laughed, stabbing at her cheeks before kneeling down beside Jen.

"Oh, honey. Jenny didn't make me cry. I was sad because I love her and I miss her when she's not here."

Allison hugged Jennifer again, her hands tucked neatly around Jen's neck. The two sisters watched each other over the top of Allison's head, a lifetime of knowing between them.

"I promise, Allison. I'll come back more often." Jen hugged her niece again before untangling herself. "And you can come and visit me too. Okay?" She tried to smile as Allison put her fist to her cheeks, rubbing her tears away. Finally, she nodded, satisfied, and Jen uncurled her knees to face her sister.

They stared at each other, fighting laughter and tears all at once, finally falling into a bear hug of emotion.

"I hate leaving. I hate good-byes," Jennifer managed.

"I hate them too," Sally growled in return. "Don't be such a stranger. I miss you."

Jennifer's throat ached. "I've missed you so much. Thanks for listening. You've been wonderful."

Sally shrugged playfully. "Yeah, well . . ." She gave her sister another quick hug. "I love you. Call me."

"Promise," Jen blinked. "I love you too." She

brushed one sleeve across her cheek and lifted a bag over one shoulder, backpedaling toward the flight attendant.

With one last look, she committed the image of her family to memory before turning on her heel and disappearing around the corner.

The plane was nearly half empty, so Jennifer made her way easily down the center aisle to her seat in row fourteen. Thankfully, no one was sitting in her row, so she placed her small bag under one of the seats and scooted over to the window seat. Granted, her ticket said that she was sitting on the aisle, but with so many empty seats on the plane, she didn't think it would matter.

She buckled her seat belt and squinted through the window, looking toward the terminal and hoping to see her sister and family there. The Des Moines airport was the only airport she'd been in where you could actually see people inside the terminal, waving to passengers onboard the plane.

But no familiar faces were in the window, and so she settled back in her seat and closed her eyes, waiting for the depression that was sure to settle over her.

She missed her sister already. Sally had been absolutely wonderful all weekend. Jen had forgotten how well they got along, how easily they talked together. If nothing else, seeing her sister had made the trip back to Des Moines worthwhile. They'd had a chance to reestablish their relationship. Jennifer vowed never to let herself put a wall up between them again.

Her thoughts roamed, settling on Heather, and she pushed the image aside. She wasn't ready to deal with those emotions yet. She thought instead of Diane and Lucy, smiling as she thought of the two of them together. She'd have to track down their address, she decided. She would definitely like to keep in touch with them.

And Sheila. Jennifer sighed, her eyes still closed, and tried to snuggle down in her seat. She wondered what was going on with Sheila and Bobby today. She wondered if Sheila was telling Bobby the truth, or if she'd continued to lie. In either case, Sheila had a tough road ahead of her, and Jennifer didn't envy her one bit.

Heather's image floated back to mind, and she held on to it this time, enjoying herself as she mentally traced over her features. She was beginning to drift, close to sleep, oblivious to the carrying-on around her, yet wondering vaguely what was holding up the flight. She was anxious to be home. She missed her animals. The horses. Her dog. She hoped that Georgie and her lover had enjoyed themselves at the ranch. She smiled a bit, thinking how Georgie wasn't all that wild about her animals.

Somewhere a child was whispering. An image of Tommy came to mind. But no, Tommy wasn't there. What a sweetie he was . . .

"Excuse me. I think you're in my daughter's seat." Someone else was talking now, the voice coming from far away, threatening to invade her sleep.

"Mommy said I can sit by the window," a child's voice was whispering in her ear. Tommy? No, the voice was too mature for Tommy. Allison. It must be Allison then.

Allison? What was she doing on the plane?

Jennifer's eyes flew open. Expecting to find Allison's brown eyes, she was surprised to find wide blue eyes staring back at her. Amy was trying not to giggle.

"Amy?" Jen lifted her sleepy eyes over the top of Amy's head to see Heather standing in the aisle beside them. She was holding a small teddy bear in one hand as a shy smile hovered on her lips.

"Heather." Jen struggled to get out of her seat, cursing the seat belt that held her firmly in place. "What are you doing here?" She managed to unclasp the buckle and found her feet. "I thought you were on a morning flight."

"We missed our flight," Heather shrugged.

"We missed the plane on purpose," Amy chimed in. As quickly as Jennifer had vacated the seat, Amy had settled into it and was strapping herself into place.

"On purpose, eh?" Jennifer grinned widely, enjoying Heather's momentary discomfort.

"Amy's imagining things," Heather lied, returning Jennifer's smile.

They stood face-to-face, with only the teddy bear in between them.

"I suppose you'll want to sit by your daughter, then," Jen said, feigning annoyance.

"And I suppose you'll want an aisle seat." Heather played along.

"Of course," Jen said.

"Of course," Heather replied.

Jennifer watched the lazy smile lifting on Heather's lips and felt her heart swelling in her chest. Slowly and casually, as if it were the most natural thing in the world, each stepped forward and into the other's arms.

"I'm so glad you're here," Jen whispered.

"I'm so sorry about last night," Heather's breath was on her ear. "I shouldn't have left like that."

"I was so worried that I wouldn't be able to find you in Flagstaff. I didn't have your address or phone number —"

The pilot's voice came over the intercom, asking the flight attendants to prepare for takeoff. Both Heather and Jennifer became aware of their surroundings, and they stepped back and rearranged themselves and their belongings as Heather settled down beside her daughter.

"Can we come to your house now and see the horses?" Amy could barely contain herself as she leaned across Heather's lap to look up at Jen.

"You're welcome to come to my house anytime," Jen smiled. "But I think that's up to your mom."

"We'll see, Amy." Heather held out the stuffed bear to her daughter. "Jenny and I have a lot to talk about first, okay?"

Amy's frown lasted only a moment. "Okay," she shrugged. She took the bear from her mother, pressing its nose beside her own to the small window.

Heather turned back to Jen as the plane began rolling backward.

"We have a lot to talk about, do we?" Jen asked. "Sounds ominous."

"I hope not," Heather laughed. "But I've got you trapped for three solid hours, and I want to hear all about what happened this weekend." Her blue eyes smoldered as they held Jen's gaze. "Your version, that is," she added.

Jennifer cringed. "You may not like it."

"No," Heather agreed. "But I want to hear it anyway. Maybe you should start back at the beginning."

"The beginning?"

Heather nodded. "Back in school. Just how did you and Sheila become lovers? How in hell did you end up as her maid of honor? And what did you ever see in her, anyway?"

Jen stopped to ponder the last question. "I don't know —"

"She was a self-absorbed snob. Pouty. Whiny. And she had you wrapped around her little finger. How did that happen? Why was she worth it?"

Again Jennifer was without an answer, and she shrugged her shoulders lamely.

"I guess you'll just have to start at the beginning then. Maybe if you don't leave anything out, I'll be able to figure out exactly what the attraction was." Heather's tone was playful, with a hint of seriousness.

Already weary of the story ahead, Jennifer said, "It's a long story."

Heather blinked her eyes and shrugged. "You've got a captive audience."

Jennifer sighed as her eyes fell over Heather's features. Her long blond hair was pulled back in a single braid, exposing a long neck that Jennifer wanted to snuggle into. Her eyes fell to the base of Heather's throat, her pulse quickened as she imagined its softness against her own lips.

Too late to turn back now. She knew she was

already in love. She relished the thought, smiling secretly. *Patience,* she said to herself. *Have patience.*

Their eyes met again, and Jennifer cleared her throat. "I swear," she began, "that this is the last time that I'll ever tell this story."

"And I swear," Heather replied in a slightly mocking tone, "that this is the last time I'll ever ask."

"Deal," Jen grinned.

"Deal," Heather smiled.

Epilogue

It was unusually hot for May, even for Phoenix. It hadn't rained in weeks, and everyone was feeling the effects of the long heat wave.

Jennifer felt irritable as she pulled a T-shirt over her head. It was nearly eight o'clock, and she'd just arrived home from the pharmacy. She'd had to put in too many hours since Jim had decided to retire.

She stepped into a pair of loose cotton shorts and padded across the bedroom floor. She reached for the screened patio door and pulled it aside before stepping out onto the veranda.

Taking a deep breath, she leaned against the wooden railing and looked over the patch of yard that led to the barn and surrounding paddock.

She hadn't paid attention to the horses or the ranch in weeks, and yet everything seemed in order. The spring grass was green — no easy accomplishment in this heat. Four of their six horses were enjoying the shade of the huge oak just inside the fence.

She could hear Banjo barking, apparently from inside the barn. Her eyes turned to focus on the tall young girl who bent over a mountain of hay, gathering up one armful after another and stepping outside to dump it beside the horses. The girl caught her eye and lifted a hand in her direction before picking up a large stick and tossing it as far as she could. Banjo was off in hot pursuit, the game well-known and established. They would go on like that for an hour.

As she surveyed the property, Jen's eyes fell to a patch of multicolored flowers, newly planted around the cacti and wildflowers to the left of the front porch.

A smile crept to her lips. She wasn't paying much attention to their home these days, but someone else was. Everything was in perfect order, in spite of her neglect.

The sun was setting, the sky becoming purple where it met the horizon in the west.

She heard the screen door slide open and then shut behind her. Without turning, she felt her lover's presence behind her.

"Are you hungry? I could make you some dinner."

"No. I'm too tired and too hot to eat," she replied quietly, still distracted. Her eyes fell again to the unidentifiable new flowers, and she gave voice to her musings.

"You planted new flowers. They're lovely."

Slender arms sneaked their way around her waist from behind, and the warmth of Heather's body sent a contented sigh through her own.

"Last week," Heather's voice was quiet.

A sigh of frustration fell from Jen's lips. "I'm never here anymore. I'm missing too much. I miss you."

"I miss you too." Heather gave her a quick squeeze and rested her chin on Jen's shoulder.

"I need to cut back. Maybe to part-time."

"Good idea."

"I don't want to spend another summer behind that counter while you and Amy have the summer off," Jen continued her rationalizing.

"We'd love to have you here more."

"Besides, another year and Amy will be off to college. Who will take care of everything around here?"

"You will."

"I mean it, honey. I'm going to do it."

Heather paused before replying. "Have you heard even a word of what I've said?"

Jen slid her a sheepish look. "No."

"I've been telling you that it's okay to cut back." She leaned forward, just enough to catch the corner of Jen's mouth in a kiss. "How many years have I been suggesting just that?"

Jennifer's smile grew. "I know. I'm finally ready now, though. It's kind of scary."

"Well I, for one, can't wait."

They watched as Amy bolted the gate that surrounded the paddock and began walking toward the house, Banjo on her heels.

Watching her approach, Jennifer couldn't help but think how much she resembled her mother. She was smiling, pulling work gloves from her hands and slapping them against one thigh to shake out the dust. Amy had taken to the ranch as if she'd been born there.

"Hey, Jen," she called out as she reached the veranda. "Are you going to be around this weekend? I noticed a few splits in the fence out back, and I could use your muscle to help fix them."

Jennifer chuckled. She felt suddenly old, remembering how many times she had carefully shown Amy how to repair fences, how to feed and groom the horses. At first she had been eager to teach Amy, to draw her in and bond with her. Before long she'd actually needed Amy's help. And now, it was Amy asking for Jen's help instead. Times were changing.

"I'll be here."

"Great." She reached down, unconsciously rubbing the top of Banjo's head. She seemed to hesitate as she cocked her head to one side and addressed her mother.

"Have you told her yet?" she inquired, her voice playful.

"Sh." Heather lifted her chin from where it rested on Jen's shoulder. "Not yet."

"Uh-oh." Jen slid a look from mother to daughter. "What are you two up to now?" she teased.

"Nothing. Nothing." Amy tried to hide her grin as she lifted both hands. "I have a final tomorrow that

I have to study for." She rolled her eyes. "So I'm heading in." She turned toward the front steps and waved. " 'Night, Jen. 'Night, Mom." She threw a wink toward her mother before patting her thigh. She turned, and Banjo leaped after her, staying at her side until they disappeared inside the house.

Jen waited until she could hear the sound of Amy's feet trudging up the stairs to her bedroom. "What was all that about?"

"Your sister called today." Heather dropped light, lingering kisses along her neck. Even after ten years, a single kiss could send ripples along Jen's skin.

"Really? And just what did she have to say?" It was almost a joke. Jennifer spoke to her sister nearly every week.

"That Allison has been badgering her again." Heather was nibbling now, causing goose bumps on Jennifer's arm. "She wants to come out for the summer."

Jennifer chuckled. "I'm not surprised. I guess I just assumed that she'd come out again this year." She lifted her hands, covering Heather's where they lay at her waist. She settled back in her lover's arms. "Is it all right with you if she comes back?"

"Of course." She lifted her lips from Jen's neck and stepped around beside her, joining her at the railing. "I know Amy can't wait to see her. And it will be good to have someone else her age around. I worry about her sometimes. She doesn't seem to have a lot of friends."

Jennifer raised an arm to wrap it around Heather's waist, gently pulling her close. "Amy's a wonderful girl. I don't think you have anything to worry about." She reached out a hand to push a strand of hair back from her lover's brow, taking a moment to look into her eyes. "She's happy, Heather."

"I know she is. But she doesn't have any special friends, really."

"She and Allison are close."

"We have the phone bill to prove it," Heather conceded, but continued her musing. "She never talks about boys, either. Does she talk about them to you?"

"Not much," Jen admitted, then she grinned. "Hey, maybe she likes —"

"Don't be a pig." Heather slapped Jen's arm playfully. "We're talking about our daughter."

"I know. I know. I just remember what I was doing when I was sixteen." She wiggled her eyebrows suggestively and grinned.

"I know what you were doing when you were sixteen. I also know whom you were doing it with," Heather retorted as she placed a well-aimed elbow to Jennifer's ribs.

Jen grimaced. "I guess maybe we shouldn't go down that road."

Heather wrinkled her nose and laughed. "No. Let's not. But that reminds me." She turned in the circle of Jen's arms, sliding her hands up to play with the thick hair that just reached the collar of Jen's T-shirt.

Jennifer eyed the other woman's playful smile, knowing she was up to no good. "Uh-oh." She squinted into twinkling eyes. "What are you up to?"

"Nothing."

"Uh-huh."

Heather laughed. "It's not me. It's your sister." She leaned forward to place a wet kiss on Jen's chin.

"She said there was a notice in the paper last Sunday."

Jen held her at arm's length, her brow pulled down with worry. "Who died? Is everything all right?"

Heather nodded, feigning seriousness. "It seems that they're looking for members of the George Washington High School class of seventy-seven."

Jen blinked, not getting the hint.

"They're having our twenty-year class reunion in August." Heather grinned, showing even white teeth. "Wanna go?"

Jennifer groaned, throwing back her head and chuckling loudly. "No way."

"Oh come on," Heather gave her a squeeze. "Sally said she had a wonderful time at her reunion last year."

"I'll bet she did," she laughed. Then she let her eyes travel over her lover's face, savoring each detail. "Has it really been ten years?"

"It has." Heather snuggled back into Jen's arms, burying her face against Jen's neck.

Jen held her tightly, a soft smile hovering on her lips as she thought of the past. "Do you remember the first time we made love?"

"Of course." Heather alternately nibbled and kissed Jen's neck. "It was right in that room." She nodded toward the open doors that led to the bedroom.

Jennifer smoothed back the hair on Heather's brow, then let her hands begin to wander. No matter how familiar she was with her lover's body, she never tired of the feel of her smooth skin beneath her fingers. "Technically, I believe the first time was out here."

Heather's hands were on Jen's breasts, and Heather heard with satisfaction the sharp intake of Jen's breath. "Are you sure about that?" She pushed the T-shirt aside and lowered her head just enough to slide her tongue across one nipple.

"P-positive." Jennifer breathed heavily with anticipation, her own hands finding skin beneath Heather's shirt.

"Hmm. I don't think so, Jenny." Her fingers and tongue continued their dance. "Do I have to remind you how it was? Where it was?" She lifted her head to look into Jen's eyes.

Jennifer gazed back from beneath lids heavy with arousal. "Uh-huh," she nodded, grinning. She leaned down, meeting Heather's lips with her own, their tongues meeting and joining and stirring familiar passion.

Their hands were wandering in earnest now, slipping inside the waistbands of each other's shorts, relishing the feel of each other's body.

"Have I told you that I love you?" Jen asked, as she often did.

"No. Not today," Heather laughed, her breath catching in her throat as Jen found the dampness between her legs.

"Well, I do," Jen whispered, suddenly quite serious. She lifted her head, and watched the growing rapture sliding across her lover's face. "I'd do anything for you, you know."

A smile touched Heather's lips; coherent thought

left her as Jennifer's fingers found her center. She struggled to open her eyes, unwilling to give in just yet.

"So we can go then?" Her lips were open, ready for Jen's kiss.

"Go where?"

"To the reunion." Her lips found Jennifer's, kissing her soundly. She was fading fast.

"Anywhere," Jen whispered against her mouth. "I'll go anywhere."

With a soft chuckle deep in her throat, Heather gave in to the pleasure, wrapping herself in the exquisite joy that was her lover.